MW01236166

EROTIC

BLOOM

*Blaque Cherie—
Thank you for your
support. It's very much
appreciated. Erotic blessings!*

*Karma Eve
3/29/2008*

KARMA EVE

First published in the United States in 2008 by

Soul Write Publishing, LLC
P.O. Box 171078
Nashville, TN 37217

ISBN: 978-0-9787857-5-8

For information on permissions or to order additional books,
please write:

Soul Write Publishing, LLC
P.O. Box 171078
Nashville, TN 37217
USA

Or visit our website and on-line catalog at
www.soulwritepublishing.com

Cover image by G. Seth West

DEDICATION

For those who are not afraid of sex no matter what
form it presents itself.
For those who are free sexually, mentally,
emotionally, and of course physically.
For those who understand sex, where it
comes from, how to use it and not abuse it.
For every woman and every man who has taken
their own personal sexual stand, grow like the
new sexual flower and bloom erotically.

Welcome to EROTIC BLOOM.

INTRODUCTION

Free your mind
Let your imagination run free
Don't be afraid of your sexuality
Cum in, lose yourself in this world of fantasy

It's intimate play at it's best.

Here is what you're feeling but only think
Here is what you're thinking but afraid to speak
Here is what you're wanting but afraid to ask

Here are your desires coming to life,
At last

A collection of erotic short stories and erotic
poems

Erotically Speaking,
Karma Eve

Table of Contents

Let's Pretend

Do u want me 2 get on my hands and knees 4 u
Then I'll do whatever pleases u

U want me to ride u from room 2 room
And make u feel like you're on the moon

Want me 2 scream out Daddy and call your name
And every time we make love never make it the same

Let me show u what a bad girl I can b
Let me give u head while you're watching TV

I'll b your freak 4 the night
I'll b your bitch if it's right
I'll make u moan and shiver until the early light

4 u I'll pretend I'm a dyke or dress like a whore
Or greet u butt naked when u walk thru the door

Look at me now I'm your human buffet
Use your tongue 2 dig in and have it your way

4get about high class when you softly slap my ass
Make it bounce, make it wiggle
Make it laugh, make it giggle
When you're out in the mall or club
I'll act like you're not my man
I'll whisper hello and slip my # in your hand

When I finish being your personal sex kitty and ho
I'll go back 2 being the lady u know

96 Degrees

96 degrees out here and I want to sit in the stillness
of the heat
on the porch
in the shade on a lawn chair
and think of you.   ;
The air is thick and hot.
Suffocating heat.
African heat.
Just too damn hot for me to be sitting on the porch.
The wind is not blowing
and I begin
to feel
my skin
get sticky, hot, moist.
I'm sitting
looking at an empty street.
Too hot for the kids to play.
I hear the air conditioning units on
running high in the homes around me.
Cars swishing pass back and forth
until I hear a familiar engine.
An engine I've grown to know over our time together.
You pull into the driveway,
park
and walk towards me with that manly walk
that makes you, you.
"It's too hot out here, let's go in."
You say, opening the door waiting for me
to peel myself from the plastic lawn chair.
As I pass you in the doorway
I encounter your masculinity.
The lust from your eyes begins to drown me.
The cool air on my bare arms and legs make my body tin-
gle as I walk into the house.

We both head up the carpeted stairs. I take them two at a time.

We head to my incense aromatized bedroom.

I'm so glad I got up early this morning to clean up.

I head to the bathroom to run water for a shower.

The water, not too hot, not too cool.

I hear you turn the television on.

Of course to the video channel, you can't live without your music.

I close the bathroom door, kick off my pink flip-flops, step out of my dark denim short-shorts, the kind with the bottom of my cheeks hanging out.

Toss my panties on the pile and remove my white tank top.

I push the shower curtain to the side and pull it back in place as I let the water envelope me.

I close my eyes and feel the rhythmic massage like patter from my indoor waterfall.

I reach for my fluffy, purple sponge and my liquid soap and I hear,

"I'll get that." Sex dripping from your voice.

I must have been in a trance from my fountain because I didn't even hear you come in.

"Damn!" I think to myself as I open my eyes and see you standing naked next to the tub.

"How did I miss my own personal strip show?" I think as you step in behind me adjusting the showerhead so some of my cascade becomes some of yours too.

Big chest,

Pressed against my back.

Thick penis,

swinging,

lightly touching my butt.

You reach for the soap, squeeze some on my purple sponge and began to wash me.

I close my eyes again and just take it all in.

You soap me down from neck to ass, where you take the
sponge and glide it softly, slowly, back and forth between
my pretty, black thighs.
Making me moan lightly.
You turn me towards you letting the spray of the water
wash the soap off my back.
You kiss me and we both get wet.
You continue to soap me as you kiss me.
My breasts love the attention.
Your kisses get deeper.
The nectar of my peach gets juicer, juicer and sweeter and
under our waterfall you take me, hungrily.
Devouring me.
Me taking you in like a newly discovered sin.
Your strong back and shoulders working as a team, elec-
trifying my body.
Picking me up, placing my body against the cool tile of
the shower wall.
Legs wrapped around your waist,
water beating down,
grabbing at you, clinging to you.
You tell me how good it is.
How deep it is, how wet it is.
"I've been wanting this all day." You say all man-ish and
stuff.
You cum
I cum
Then we actually shower
together.
But the truth is
it's 96 degrees and I'm sitting in the stillness
of the heat
on the porch
in the shade
on the lawn chair
and thinking of you.

Fantasy

I rushed to my car from work trying to stay dry from the heavy rain. "Working this late shift is so ugly." I thought as I jumped in the front seat and closed the door. I flipped the visor down to look in the mirror to see how much damage had been done to my hair. "Now that's ugly, not a curl in sight. Forget it." I said as I started the car. I backed out of the parking space and fastened my seatbelt at the same time. I pulled onto English Avenue, headed for home and turned the radio on to the late night slow jam show with D.J. Shy-Guy on WLUV 103.2. Shy-Guy's smooth, sexy voice came across the airwaves and filled the car.

"Welcome back everyone," Shy-Guy spoke. "Tonight we're talking about fantasies. What is one of your fantasies and have you ever acted it out? If not, what's stopping you? Let's go to the phones and take some calls. Hello, caller," Shy-Guy said in that mellow voice of his. "Tell me all about your fantasy."

As the caller began to speak about his fantasy that involved Mrs. Butterworth syrup and two women, I began to have thoughts myself. "This is the perfect time to do it," I said aloud.

A few minutes later I pulled in front of the apartment and I could see the glow of the television through the upstairs blinds. When I entered our place, all the lights were out so I used the light from the television to lead me upstairs. There he was, curled up on his side like a baby, sound asleep. Whenever it rains I can expect him to be asleep. "I hope this works." I whispered to myself while slipping off my athletic shoes and socks. I got out of the clothes I wore to work and threw on some old shorts, shirt and slid my feet into some slide-on shoes. "Wake up, sleepyhead. Let's go," I whispered in his ear. After shaking him several times, I finally got a response.

"What?" He asked sounding irritated.

"Let's go." I said again.

"Go where? What time is it?"

I looked at the digital clock that sat on the nightstand.

"It's 1:35."

"In the morning?" he asked shocked.

"Just trust me Anthony and come on. We don't have all night." I pulled him out of bed. "Trust me." Surprisingly he got out of bed with no more questions and slipped on his house shoes.

"Veronica, where are we going?" He asked now sitting on the side of the bed looking at an old I Love Lucy rerun and trying to collect his thoughts.

"To paradise."

"I can't believe you got me out in the rain at this time of morning. Baby this better be good."

He closed his eyes and leaned his head back against the seat. I just giggled and turned up the radio. The Isley Brothers' In Between the Sheets was playing. "Well, no sheets tonight." I said to myself. The rain was still coming down steadily. I took McCallister Road until it turned into Highway 10, the more country side of town. There were more spaces between houses and plenty of land and fields. I drove for just a few minutes more and pulled off to a side rode. Off to the side of the road was a grassy field. I brought the car to a crawl as I surveyed the area and listened to another caller talking to D.J. Shy-Guy. This caller was saying how her fantasy failed with her, her now ex-boyfriend and her ex-best friend. "Bad move girl." I said as I brought the car to a stop. I turned off the engine, the lights and the wipers. I left the radio on and increased the volume. I slipped off my shoes and opened the car door. The footlights came on and the ding sound from the door being opened woke him out of his nap.

12

"Come on." I said stepping out and feeling the soft, wet combination of grass and earth sink beneath my feet. I sat on the front hood of the car and felt its warmth beneath me. The rain was coming down in big quarter shaped drops that felt like the cooler version of a warm, relaxing shower. Light steam was slowly rising from the hood and my t-shirt and boxer style shorts were getting soaked. I laid back, closed my eyes and let the rain take me in its arms. I then heard the ding sound from the car door being opened. Excitement slowly begins to build within me. The car slightly went down as he got on the hood with me. I felt his lips on mine, wet from the rain, his tongue eagerly searching for mine. He slowly rolled on top of me kissing me all over my face tenderly and sweet, licking my neck and lifting up my shirt to get to my breasts and waiting nipples. I slid the shirt over my wet hair and let it fall behind us on the windshield. Our eyes had adjusted to the darkness because I could see him staring at me through the rain. I let him pull off my shorts and lacey peach colored panties. I pulled his soaked shirt over his head and threw it behind me. He took off his boxer shorts and I noticed immediately how excited he had become. I watched the rain dance over his well-formed body. He then reached for my legs and gently pulled me towards him. He slowly kissed and caressed each breast giving special attention to my nipples, which were hard like stones. Licking down to my navel, letting his tongue play with my navel ring. Down into a new land, past the soft hair-like silky trees, his tongue searched the soul of my wetness. Taking his time, he licked my inner thighs, kissed my hips, licked my stomach and fondled my breasts. Reaching my ear and whispering heavily, "I want you." He then carefully guided himself into a wet wonderland, with me taking him in and whispering a low sultry, "Yes, oh yes." Our hips rotated and gyrated. The rain beat on his back like a drum-

mer in a parade. It covered my face like a see through
veil. The sounds of pleasure filling the warm, stormy
night air. Flesh on top of flesh, gripping hands, the taste
of his skin and rain on my tongue was like a chocolate
raindrop surprise. I could feel his excitement building
within me, his hot, stiff dick going in and out and in and
out of my wet, tight pussy, giving me lustful pleasure
with each motion. In between sex filled moans and
groans we switched positions with ease. I was on top of
him, the rain dripping from my hair down my back. In
the darkness I could see his face twisting with sweet ecstasy. I slowly lifted myself up just enough to have the
tip of his hard dick right at the opening of my hot, waiting pussy. I slowly lowered myself onto him. Slowly,
slowly, slowly. With each move taking him to a higher
level of excitement. Riding him with great pleasure and
much force. Our bodies fitting together like pieces to a
puzzle. The sounds of ecstasy and nature flowing
throughout the field, above us and around us, surround-
ing our beautiful brown naked bodies like a blanket.
Licking, kissing, feeling. Touching, hugging, gripping.
Holding tight, moaning. Going faster, faster, faster, keeping in rhythm. Our excitement building. Tension mount-
ing. Sensations tingling, up and down, up and down.
The climax climbing, going to the edge, holding onto the
edge, not wanting to go over, not wanting to let go.
Hanging on. Listening to his heavy breathing. Hanging
on. Feeling him plunge deeper with every thrust inside
me. Hanging on. Feeling my wetness coming down,
coming down. "I'm cumming!" I scream out with a raspy
voice. "I'm cumming!" I repeated. I hear him moan, I
feel him shudder, I see him tremble. He grabbed me,
held me. He pulled me so close I laid on him breast to
chest, both of us trying to catch our breath. I felt him inside me slightly throbbing, lightly going limp.
The rain begins to ease up, nice, light, drops. Laying

there for a few moments, we then began to collect our wet clothes. Slipping back into the car and hearing En Vogue's Giving Him Something He Can Feel, I laughed to myself.

"Baby, that was the greatest," he said leaning over and kissing me on the lips.

I pull up in front of the apartment, run in from the rain and for a moment just standing with my back to the door, listening to the silence of the house. Coming home to an empty, dark place, no one here, just the quietness of the house.

"Just a fantasy." I say out loud. "It was all just a fantasy."

Fuck

I've been known to love hard
But those who know me, know me well
I fuck hard so I can have a tale to tell

You know how Tom Joyner parties with a purpose?
I fuck with a plan
I fuck on a mission
I fuck with a vengeance
I fuck for all those you can't fuck
For the ones too old to give a fuck
I fuck for all of those who's never had that BIG orgasmic
firework lighting up the inside of their souls
BOOM!
POP!
POW!

I fuck for all those who thought they were getting it
served up on a silver platter
Only to find out it was served cold in one of those old,
blue Styrofoam McDonald filet-o-fish boxes

I do it for all those who are born again virgins with 3 kids
by 4 baby daddies
You know, that Maury Povich
"You-are-not-the-father" shit
Cause she just ain't going through that shit again

I fuck for the ones who are afraid to touch and fuck themselves
BULLSHIT!

I fuck so good, if I fuck myself I gotta be careful 'cause I'll
find myself falling in love with me and asking me to
marry myself so we can settle down and become we and

when me says no, I'm afraid I'll stalk me and me will
have to call the police on myself and have us arrested.
Damn! That's just way too far

I fuck back and forth
I fuck smooth
YOU want to be fucked by me
You want to be surrounded and swimming in my fuck
How can something so simple be so hypnotic?
Like the waves of the ocean
Then I slam you down, mount on top and ride you fever-
ishly with that ghetto motion

I'm the Fuck Princess
The Fuck Queen
Fuck it
I'm the Fuck Goddess

So the next time you wanna get down
Get dirty
Get raw
Get kinky
Get your rocks off
You know what the fuck to do
Come see me, 'cause whatever's good for me
I'm sho nuff gonna make sure it's good for you

Pure

Damn, here I am with some of the best sex in the world
and no real man to give it to.
I mean I can't give my treasure away to just any man.
No disrespect to ANY man within ear shot,
I know you're a strong brotha in your own right and I
would love for you to receive this pleasure morning,
noon and night.
But all you well-hung, hittin' deep, puttin' your lover to
sleep brothas, get comfortable while I introduce you to
real sex.
Pure sex.
My sex.

See I have that liquid Tide sex.
You know, that concentrated sex, where a little bit goes a
long way.
It's more than physical.
It's emotional.
Mental,
And in the name of the Father,
The Son and Holy...
Oops!
Yeah, I mean it's spiritual.
It's true.
It's natural, soul-on-fire,
Reaching new heights and levels and never wanting to
come down off the high I give type of sex.
The nose bleed,
Light-headed,
Getting dizzy and nauseous type of sex.
My sex will make a man go to the East Side of the Gar-
den,
Pick a piece of fruit from the forbidden tree,
Take a bite and tell Satan,

18

"Take my house, my car and all my clothes. Cut me open and take my Soul. Just allow me access to that pure sex!"

My sex is so deep if I gave a million men, a million shovels to dig their way to the end, they'd be like the missing soldiers of a war long forgotten.
Instead of being M.I.A. they'd be considered M.I.K.S.
Missing In Karma's Sex (or insert your own name if this applies to you)

Sex with me is crazy, strong, steady, unforgotten, meaningful.
(Gasp) You feel that? That quivering?
That means a man somewhere who has had sex with me just thought about an act we performed and trembled like a bitch being slapped by her pimp.
How touching.
They can feel me in the air they breathe and the water they drink.
That's my sex.
I'm not afraid of it and don't you be.
You have to be of sound mind (Ohm)
And body
To be the dog to catch this cat.
Take this as a lesson to be learned,
This here is some fire pussy that has to be earned.
Now that you're aware of what you're getting into
To be the lucky man to make my muscles flex,
Come and get it,
Only if you can handle it,
100 Percent
Uninhibited
Adult
Pure sex.

The Confession

"Sorry I'm late," Reverend Spencer said as he led me into his office.

"That's all right, I'm not in any hurry." What I needed to discuss was embarrassing not only to me but would kill Darren if he knew I was here talking about it. Since I'd never been in Rev. Spencer's office, I didn't know what to expect, but what I did see was very nice.

"Your office is very nice and quite comfortable," I told him. Rev. Spencer had a pretty big office. It was beautifully decorated with large African masks and pictures. A huge mahogany desk and matching curio cabinet filled with African artifacts were on one side of the room. On the other side of the room was a comfortable looking plush couch and in front of it was a large African style drum wrapped with lion cloth that he displayed as a coffee table. He also had various live hanging plants and potted trees throughout the office. It gave the office such an exotic look and feel.

"Thank you, Veronica. Some of the things you see are from my travels and others are from members of the church as gifts."

I was very impressed with what I saw.

"Please, have a seat," he said as he walked around his desk to have a seat in his big, dark leather chair. "So, what can I do for you today?" he asked folding his hands like a steeple under his chin and resting his elbows on the desk.

I really wish I could have put this off longer, but I'm here in front of him so I might as well go for it. "I can't believe I'm saying this, but I don't think I want to marry Darren." I squeezed my eyes tightly, held my breath and waited for his response.

"What?" he said loudly.

I opened one eye to see a shocked Reverend staring

back at me.

"What do you mean you don't think you want to marry Darren?" he asked still with a shocked expression. "You and Darren were just in last month for your pre-marital counseling sessions and I couldn't recommend a more perfect couple to get married.

"I know, Rev. Spencer, but..." My voice trailed off. I was too ashamed to just come out and say it.

"Veronica, but what?" he asked leaning forward and looking concerned.

"Is Darren seeing someone else?"

"No!" I looked down at my hands in my lap.

"Oh my goodness! Has that boy hit you?" Rev. Spencer became angry.

"No, Reverend, nothing like that," I quickly answered.

"Then what is it? He's providing for you, isn't he?"

"Yes, very much," thinking of how giving Darren was made this even harder.

Rev. Spencerleaned back into his chair, took in a deep breath and slowly folded his arms across his chest. He looked me straight in my eyes and asked in a low, soft voice, "Veronica, what's the problem? I can't help you if I don't know what the problem is."

Rev. Spencerwas a very handsome man. He stood about six feet two inches and looked even taller when he preached. His skin was as dark as midnight and smooth as the dark wood on his desk. He had a very calm and quiet manner until he was in the pulpit and spoke from the pit of his soul. Then he became a thunderous, booming voice spewing out words of wisdom and filling everyone's spiritual appetite. Even though Rev. Spencerwas just a few years older than me, in his early forties, as I looked at him he had such a powerful hold over me.

"What could be so bad that you want to call off the wedding, Veronica?" He broke my concentration.

I answered softly. "The sex."

21

"I'm sorry, I didn't hear you." He now leaned forward.

"The sex." I said again looking off around the room.

"Oh!" was all the Reverend could say.

"I just don't know what to do." I rambled off. "Darren is a good man. He gives me everything I need and even things I don't think I need." I then fingered the diamond tennis bracelet on my left wrist he gave me just two nights ago at dinner. "We have such a wonderful time together and I love him with all of my heart. The only thing is when it comes to making love, Darren is clueless and I can't see myself not being pleased sexually for the rest of my life."

The Reverend sat stunned. "I'm speechless, I must say. I truly wasn't expecting this."

I continued. "I've tried everything. His technique is awful." I frowned.

The Reverend chuckled. I began to cry.

"Oh, Veronica, I'm sorry." He got up to come from behind his desk. "I didn't mean to laugh." He hugged me. The smell of his cologne was soothing and his comforting arms around me felt so good. I dried my eyes with a tissue the Reverend handed me from a box on his desk. We stood there embracing for a moment and not saying anything.

"Does Darren know how you feel?"

"That's all we fight about. In fact, it's the only thing we fight about." We finally let go of one another even though I could have held on forever.

"What does he say about this situation?" Rev. Spencer asked sitting on top of his desk.

"Darren doesn't think there is a problem. He gets what he can get and doesn't satisfy me."

"That's not good. I see how this can be frustrating for you." He let out a sigh.

"There is no passion in our love life. He doesn't hold me, cuddle, use foreplay, nothing that makes me feel spe cial." I was getting angry just thinking about it.

Rev. Spencer sat thinking. "Would you like me to get you both back here in my office to address this situation?"

I was confused, frustrated and in need of some good sex. I looked at the Reverend and felt an overwhelming urge to have him right then and there.

"No, Reverend I don't think that will be necessary." I gently placed my hand on the inner part of his thigh. He was still very much active in sports. His body showed the results. I'd heard him say several times that he played basketball on a small league consisting of other pastors and deacons from area churches. He's also spoke of participating in boxing. Whatever he does it sure keeps him looking fine. I looked deep into his dark brown eyes as I got closer to him. His cologne was like a magnet pulling me in and my body ached for his touch. I'm sure he felt what I was feeling. He hadn't removed my hand and he waited quietly as I made my move. Just as I was leaning in for a kiss, the phone on his desk rang. We both were startled.

"Yes, Gloria," he tried to sound normal. "That's fine, Gloria. Lock the main office door when you leave and call me at home when you get more information." He listened as she spoke. "Glo, just keep calm and since this is my last appointment, don't worry about tomorrow's schedule. I'll look at the calendar when I leave. You just get going and call me later."

After getting off of the phone with his secretary, Gloria, he explained she had an emergency with her 16-year-old grandson who stayed in trouble. Any other time I would have been concerned about the situation, but at this moment my body was on fire and screaming for attention. "I'm your last appointment for the evening?" I asked in a whisper.

"Yes, you are and my secretary is locking the main office doors as she leaves." He then put his hands around my waist and slowly pulled me closer to him. I was now standing between his legs as he continued sitting on his desk.

"Now what were you saying before the phone rang?" he questioned looking through me and at my soul. He gripped my waist tighter.

"I wasn't saying anything. It was actually what I was going to do." Before he could answer and definitely before I chickened out, I kissed him. He responded with a deep, passionate kiss that started my juices flowing. I haven't felt this light-headed and full of sexual flames since before Darren and I became involved. I undid his tie, unbuttoned his shirt and ran my hands across his strong, manly chest. Rev. Spencer untied the thin belt on my dress and slid the sleeves off my shoulders. My dress fell in a heap to the floor and I stood in front of him look-ing sexy in my matching black lace bra and panty set with my three inch black heels that fastened around my ankle.

"Lord have mercy," Rev. Spencer said softly licking his lips and looking my body up and down.

"Let's move this to the couch." he insisted taking me by the hand and leading me across the room. He removed his shoes and the rest of his clothes as I got ready to un-strap and remove my high heels.

"No, leave those on," he instructed.

The Reverend was a bit freaky and I liked it. I posi-tioned myself comfortably on the couch.

"Rev. Spencer, are you okay with this?" I wanted to make sure he wasn't having second thoughts or in the middle of us sexing each other down, he break out in a prayer.

"Veronica, please call me Terence and yes I'm very much okay with this." he laid on top of me and began smothering my body with hot, passionate kisses. Smoothly he removed my bra and with one hand fondled a breast and the other breast he slowly sucked on, slowly

24

pulling and teasing my hard nipples. I moaned with pleasure. My body hadn't felt this way in a long time. Terence's touch was so gentle, his body firm and his scent seeped passed his cologne and hypnotized me. My panties were slowly slipped off and Reverend, I mean Terence kissed down my body until he reached my sweet river flow. His tongue circled my waiting clit again and again. I realized I was holding my breath as his tongue explored my inner jewel. Taking his time, he kissed his way back up my hot body. Kissing and licking me on all my exposed tingling skin. Licking and sucking my neck, my lips, my ears. Caressing my breasts ever so gently. I was feeling so good I didn't think it could get any better. Boy was I wrong. I then felt Terence's tool of love enter my heavenly paradise and I couldn't contain my emotions. With each thrust he gave I couldn't hold back my moans. I took what he had to offer and wrapped my legs around his body tightly as I licked and moistened my dry lips. His body was powerful and it dripped with sweat while he rocked my world.

"Is this what you've been needing?" he asked as my body continued to beg for more.

"Yes, yes!" I moaned with juices bubbling between my hot thighs.

He lifted my leg over his shoulder and plunged his thick dick deeper. He hit my spot fast.

"You like that, Veronica?" He asked focused on how my body was reacting to his touch.

"Yes!" I screamed. "Keep doing it!" I instructed. Moaning uncontrollably and breathing heavily, my love hole started gripping his handle and sweet juices flowed all over Terence. No sooner after I came, Terence let loose and came too. I hadn't had an orgasm like that in so long I became dizzy. Catching our breath Terence began kissing me on my face, my neck and slowly and gently sucking my nipples. I became aroused and transfixed under his touch. My twat started stirring and apparently something in Terence started stirring too. He grinded his hips into me and I knew the blood had made it back to his dick since I felt it prodding me in my leg.

"Are you ready for round two?" he asked staring me in my eyes. The Reverend was getting ready to lay hands on my body again.

"Of course, I haven't had it this good in a long time." I replied with a sly smile.

He threw one of his pillows from the couch on the floor and told me to get on my knees and put my elbows on the pillow. I followed his instructions. He stood up behind me, took both of my ankles in each hand and sunk his big dick into my anxiously awaiting pussy. Damn! This was sheer ecstasy. In this position it allowed him to get in me deeper than any man ever has before. The blood rushing to my head made the experience ever greater. I submitted to his raunchy ways as my big, juicy ass bounced back on him. He did it to me in that position until we came once again. This time I came harder with force from way back. After Terence came, he was the first to speak.

"It looked like you enjoyed yourself."

I laughed with the mixed emotions of embarrassment and satisfaction.

"I did, but I don't think I'm the only one."

Terence had pleasured me in ways Darren couldn't even imagine. Terence started another round of our spiritual-fuck session. I was able to release tension that had built up in me from day one with Darren and I was feeling on cloud nine when Terence and I finished.

I did go through with the wedding and Darren was none the wiser about my visit with Terence, er, Rev. Spencer that day. Rev. Spencer officiated our wedding and I was probably the only bride who couldn't wait to get home from her honeymoon. Of course I had to continue seeing Terence. Darren hadn't improved in pleasing me at all. I love Darren but I have to get mine too.

God bless my soul.

If Only

Your imagination can be a motherfucker when you ain't
got nobody to slip you the dick
I lay here naked after a bath under the covers between
my clean sheets wishing he was here
I'm suppose to be sleep as my hands travel and find their
way to my phat (pretty hot and tempting) pussy

Freshly waxed
The skin where the hair used to be feels soft and smooth
The lips of my pussy more exposed than when it was cov-
ered with the love shag
I slowly rub my middle finger up and down my sensitive
clit as my pussy gets wet and the tingling sensation be-
gins
Eyes closed, lips slightly parted, silent rhythmic breaths
and my mind focuses on you
Damn! I wish you were here
I part my legs a little more and dig my fingers in deep,
pretending it's you
Slowly,
Gently,
Anxiously entering me
I take a deep breath, then slowly release it
I feel you glide in and out giving me pleasure, making me
moan
Neither one of us ready to cum yet

We switch to another position
I roll onto my knees which places you underneath me
To make this more realistic, like you're really here,
I retrieve my battery operated real-like vibrator
This time I don't turn it on
I squat over you
Insert you into me and bounce,

Bounce, bounce
Head back
Breasts flopping
Still wishing you were here to grab my waist, guide my
hips and firmly spread my ass
Juicy sounds, moaning, gasping for air
Feeling your balls slap my ass when I slam back down on
top of you
I feel it in the pit of my stomach
Even though my knees feel cramped, I can't stop
I have to continue because you're bringing me to great
heights

My moans grow louder
My back arched
My bounces becoming more aggressive
Moving faster, deeper
It happens

My mouth opens, but no sound comes out
I throw my head back as I thrust, thrust, thrust
My vibrator is wet
Dripping wet
I let out a high pitch cry and tremble
I fall face first into the pillows

Catching my breath and stretching my legs as I move my
vibrator to the other side of my empty bed
Getting comfortable, covering myself back up so I can fall
asleep
Fall into a deeper sleep
There's no other sleep like post masturbation sleep and
my body feels good
As I drift off I wonder what will I dream of tonight and
think,
If only you were here

In the Middle of the Night

In the middle of the night
I place my hands where yours would be
And imagine your lips all over me

In the middle of the night
I play with my clit and get myself wet
While thinking of the things I haven't done to you yet

You've become more than a friend
You're now apart of my fantasy world
And it's just that, a fantasy
Since in reality I'll never be your girl

In the middle of the night
I think of all the things I can never be for you
But in the middle of the night
I think of all the things I can do to you

It's in the middle of the night
Where I'll remove your clothes slowly
Piece by piece where once we begin
The action won't cease

It's in the middle of the night
Where my tongue will explore
Your body, you being a man
And so much more

In the middle of the night
Of course by candlelight
I want to screw, fuck, make love
To you
Welcome you to the height of ecstasy
Then bring you back down ever so gently

In the middle of the night
As I sleep
I part my legs slightly as I dream you're going deep
Your name comes across my lips from somewhere within
I whisper it passionately over and over again
All of this keeps my mind running free
Sets my soul on fire

I'm pleased you're what I desire
It's my fantasy
My reality
It's all about you
It's all about me
It's wrong
It's right
But only you know what happens with me
In the middle of the night

M'Bation

When I was 12-years-old I used to love to spy on my
16-year-old brother Larry and his two friends, A.J. and
Stanley. Whatever information I would find out, depend-
ing on how good it was I would use it to blackmail one of
them. Like the one time Larry tried to steal from the corner store and was caught by the owner, Mr. Phillips. Mr.
Phillips knew momma quite well and told Larry he
wouldn't tell on him if Larry promised to come to the
store everyday after school for a month to stock and clean
it. Larry of course kept his promise. I, of course found
out and told Larry if he didn't bring me some candy
home whenever I asked, I was going to tell momma.
Well, momma never found out, Mr. Phillips had a good
worker for a month and I got my candy.

One Saturday I woke up in a spying mood, but Larry,
A.J. and Stanley were nowhere to be found.
"Where did Larry go?" I asked momma.
"Serena, you are not going to bother those boys today.
Go play with some of your own friends."
I couldn't believe momma was holding out for them.
I'd find something of Larry's to get into. After eating
breakfast, I made sure momma was too deep into her
house cleaning to notice me. I decided to go into Larry's
room to see if he added anything new that I needed to
know about. I closed the door behind me as I entered.
Even though I hadn't been in his room for awhile, everything still looked the same. Messy. Fortunately I knew
where Larry's secret hiding places were and began my
search. After ten minutes of searching I was coming up
empty handed. I was ready to leave when I noticed a
brown box peeking out from behind his curtains.
"How did I miss you?" I asked in a whisper. I sat on
the floor with the box in my lap. I removed the lid and

there were about fifteen nudie magazines inside.

"Awww! Larry is gonna get it if momma finds these." I smiled to myself. I looked at all of the covers of the magazines. Each one was different. There were black people, white people, men and women on some of the covers. On others there were even women with women. I picked out one magazine that seemed the most interesting and began looking at the pictures and I even skimmed through some of the articles. From that moment on, I read and learned everything I could about sex.

That was eleven years ago and since that first time of finding Larry's dirty magazines I became known as "The Sexpert" to my two closet friends, Kim and Tamika. I learned how to have multiple orgasms, suck a dick, make his toes curl and scream out, "You're the goddess of love," all at the same time. Of all the sex techniques I've learned the one lesson I love and give two thumbs up to, is how to please myself. That's right. The wonderful art of masturbation.

"Get to know you."

"Don't be afraid to explore the inner you."

"Love you from the inside out."

"Make love to you, like no one else can." The various articles advised me.

Believe me, I followed all the rules. Kim and Tamika were always wearing their hair a certain way, wearing certain perfumes, and certain designer clothes all for the sake of whatever man that was in their lives. Me? I was so addicted to self-love, I did all of those things for me, not some man. I also worked out five days a week to keep the fullness of my breasts, the tightness in my abs, the firmness in my ass and the all over definition for my viewing pleasure. I pamper me better than any man could. Manicures, pedicures, facials, body wraps, anything that makes my body feel good. I see my body as an

Egyptian temple, sacred and precious. Some evenings after work I come home and treat myself to a night of self-satisfaction. On nights when I feel like a good girl, I'll fix dinner, open a bottle of wine, turn on some slow jams and get into a hot bath with bubbles. After relaxing in the tub for about twenty minutes or so, I get out, put on a body moisturizer and slip on something pretty and feminine. I then get in bed, turn on the television and begin to play in my treasure of joy. With my legs spread slightly, one hand slowly massaging my pretty, pink clit, the other hand rubs my breasts until each nipple is at complete attention. When my love nest becomes wet, I slowly insert one finger in and out then two fingers and continue to let my thumb massage my pink button, keeping it alert and ready. Moving my fingers in and out in a slow motion rhythm, I feel the warm sensation of wine and sex running through my body. Under the comforter the sexual desire becomes intense with every feel, every thrust, every pull. The slow burning heat rises, I arch my back and let out a soft cry as I release my flow. I feel the inner, moistness of myself grasping then releasing my fingers. It does it again and again and again until I moan and shiver with sexual happiness. When it's over I suck my thumb like a full and happy infant. I drift off to sleep in my personal pool of milk and honey.

On those nights when I feel like a bad girl, like tonight, all I can say is watch out. I come out of all of my clothes from the time I enter the house until I reach my bedroom. I put on an outfit that I've ordered from the catalog that has to be delivered in a plain envelope. My selection tonight is a very simple peek-a-boo bra, crotch less panties and six inch stiletto heels. Everything in black. I look at my delicious light caramel body in the full length mirror and I love the image looking back at me. I would tell myself "you go girl" but the girl has gone and come back again. I pull out the bottom drawer of my jewelry box and get out a nicely rolled joint. I light it up, take a few hits and glide to the kitchen to pour myself a glass of white wine. I go back to the bedroom, turn on some jazz and get in my black leather lounge chair. For some added fun I decided to call Collin. Collin is a lawyer originally from D.C. who under those expensive suits he wears in court is nothing but a freak in heat. The phone rang twice before he answered. "Hello?" He has a deep, sexy voice like the character Kyle Barker from the sitcom Living Single.

"Do you have time for one round of fun?" I asked without identifying myself.

"Serena, I always have time for you, my exotic love-bird."

I giggled feeling the wine and weed mixing within me. "Good!" I replied.

Collin was the only male I trusted to tell about my love for masturbation. He understands me and is always ready to accommodate me and play my games. With Collin, we can play in person or over the phone. It's always my choice. I settled back in my chair and closed my eyes.

"You have perfect timing. I just came in from playing basketball at the gym."

I imaged his well toned body running up and down the basketball court.

"That means you're all sweaty and worked up, just how I like you."

He quickly replied, "And you're all worked up, just how I like you."

Collin is six feet five inches, medium complexion with that good grade of hair. He has gorgeous hazel colored eyes and a sexy thin mustache. He works out five to six days a week either at the health club or his personal home gym. He makes Shemar Moore look like a lost clown

35

separated from the circus. He is one of the few men that brings me great sexual satisfaction.

"What are you wearing?" he asked in his low sexy voice.

"Tonight I went with simplicity with a touch of hard edge and rough play. I have on a black bra that exposes my juicy, erect nipples you love to suck. I'm also wearing black, crotch less panties that currently have the aroma of sweet pussy filling the air. For footwear I have chosen a sexy six inch stiletto that accentuates my beautiful legs you love to wrap around you and it shows off my expensively manicured toes you love to suck which are painted in a color called 'Jazzy Heart Red.'"

I could hear his breathing pattern change from calm to excited.

"I bet you look sexy," he commented.

"Trust me sweetheart, I do."

The conversation went into the real reason for me calling and within moments Collin's sensuous voice had me climaxing and dripping my flow all in my leather chair. After we both caught our breath, we promised to get together later in the week for a little face to face action. I relit my joint still feeling the need to call on Large Richard to take me into this next round. I went to the back of my closet and there he was, my Large Richard. He's also known as my Big Dick. Big Dick is a super sized dildo that I bring out for those really horny nights. I took Dick out of his storage container and got on the floor in front of my full length mirror. Seeing my reflection made my pussy throb with pleasure. I began playing with Dick rubbing him all over my body to make us feel as one. I slowly inserted the head into my mouth and looked in the mirror to see my thick, juicy lips going up and down the life-like shaft. My head bobbed up and down. I wanted to take my game to the next level. I reached into a nearby nightstand and pulled out a miniature vibrator that I gently inserted in my tight ass. I laid still taking in this exotic view in the mirror, opened my legs to get a look at my wet, perfectly waxed pussy and put Dick to work. I alternated Dick and the vibrator, making sure both holes were filled and satisfied. I continued that sexual task long enough to get loosened up. I then laid Dick to the side and got on my knees to give my full attention to the vibrator in my pretty caramel colored ass. I saw myself in the mirror, reached back for the base of the vibrator where I gently pulled it out and slowly pushed it back in. I started talking to myself as I felt the constant buzz fucking my ass.

"Look at you, you horny bitch. Take it in the ass you sexy bitch. You know you like it. Oh yeah baby, you know you look good."

My swollen brown breasts swung back and forth making me even hornier. I continued cursing and complimenting myself at the same time. After awhile my body began to shake as I yelled, "Yes, yes, yes!"

I had a small climax but I wasn't finished yet. I took a drink of my wine to moisten my dry mouth. "Final round." I said grabbing for Big Dick. I lay in Big Dick's favorite position, on my back and inserted Dick like an inexperienced virgin. I was still wet, so pushing him in was easy even though he was longer and wider than the average man's love wand. "Mmm." I used both hands to position him just how I liked him. The deeper I went with my thrust the closer I got to my climax. Deep and steady is the pace I chose to use. I rotated my hips getting the pleasure I wanted from my imaginary lover. "Push it deeper. Fuck this dick." I pushed him in until he was touching my special spot. My mouth opened but nothing came out. The energy was building, my pussy was feeling good, and I was fucking faster and harder. My breasts were rapidly moving back and forth. My throat was dry due to my hard and heavy breathing. Be-

37

fore I knew it, my body grew stiff then weak, but I continued fucking. It felt so good to have that wet and warm sensation between my thighs. I closed my eyes and arched my back letting all my juices flow. I let out quick breaths trying to control and steady myself. Gradually I came back down to earth feeling very much satisfied. Gathering all my senses I looked at the digital clock on the nightstand. It was almost time for the news. I decided to take a shower before I got in bed. I had a busy day tomorrow but I was already planning to take time out for a quickie. I'm never too busy for self-satisfaction. As I entered the bathroom and began running the water for my shower, I thought how I could take a long lunch, come home and work in some "self love". I smiled as I adjusted the water and let my imagination wander.

Wicked Nastiness

Black sex
Deep sex
Rock, rock rockin' the bed sex
Knockin' the boots kind of sex.
Wild sex
Hot sex
Startin' internal fire sex.
Sweatin' out my hairdo
Funkin' up my room Boo.
Fuckin' me out the bed sex
Damn near breakin' my neck sex.
Got a cramp in my foot, now it's in my leg sex
Rub it out and keep pumpin' sex
Rub again but keep humpin' sex.
Slap my ass and slap it hard sex
My head is bob, bob, bobbin' against the wall sex.
I called you a name
You called me a name.
I scratched yo' back
You scratched back but it ain't the same.
Flippin sex
Acrobatic sex
Positioned in front of you on my knees suckin dick sex.
Takin' it from the rear sex.
Whisperin' in my ear what's next.
Pounding it in, driving it home
Jack hammer sex.
I'm coachin' you on,
"Come on baby give it to momma" sex.
Callin' out my name
St-st-stutterin' like you in pain sex.
Drippin' sweat
Gettin' what you can get
We ain't finished yet

'Cause the pussy is still wet.
Grip the sheets,
Grind to the beat,
We nasty like 2 dogs in heat, during Summer in the middle of the street.
Now it's my turn to let it burn.
Let it loose, what's the use
to hold it in, we're more than friends.
Messin' with the brain, going insane
This passion is hot as flames, sex.
Wakin' the neighbors with all kinds of noise, sex.
You can't get this from none of yo' boys sex.
Well,
Maybe you can.
I hope that ain't cho plan.
If you're on the D. L. quit creepin' with a man, sex!
Breathin' heavy
Hot and heavy
Heavy and hot.
We're breathin' hard sex
Hardly breathin' sex.
Muscles flexin'
Doin' it hard, doin' it long,
Strokin' me strong, of course all night long, sex.
Here's a nut
There's a nut
All over my back and butt, sex.
Are you crazy or what?
You ain't done 'cause of that nut!
Lick between my pretty thighs
Lick my wetness dry sex,
Damn near 'til I cry sex.
Come up for air with your face wet,
Did you eat all you could eat sex?
Now come up on top and hit it again
Make me lose my voice.

Grab for things that ain't even there
Stroke and pull and scratch my hair.
That turns me on, sex.
I'm cummin' all over your manly thang and you're cum-
min' all up in me.
Our glistenin' bodies from the sweat we wear,
Twisted, crumpled sheets.
Coolin' off
Comin' down from a wild, raw sexual ride.
We smacked it,
Flipped it,
and honey dipped it.
With my pretty pussy and your delicious dick,
It's all just too damn wicked
SEX!

Thunder Cat

I got that hot sex
Loud sex
Do it 'til we're raw sex
If we've never done it, you want to find out if you're next
sex

I know you want to know how I got it like that
Because I have the pussy
Of a Thunder Cat
Pretty and black with fur all soft
Fucking with me you're guaranteed to get off

I got that hard sex
Rough sex
Doing it like it's grimy sex

It's the spirit of the Thunder Cat that brings out the fight
Can't calm it with Ritlin
'Cause it's too damn hype

When the cat was just a kitten, we didn't know what it
could do
But now it's grown and out the jungle and always in pur-
suit
Constantly on a manhunt and creeping for new prey
Lay down, give in to Thunder Cat or get the fuck up out
the way

I got that gushy sex
Drowning sex
For real, sho' nuff the pussy's wet, sex

The Thunder Cat will make you roar
Bringing satisfaction and so much more

Either bow down or throw rose petals, just respect this cat
Treat it like royalty and I'm the Queen, yeah, I like it like
that

Now that you know how me and my pussy flow
If you need us just holla,
Thunder,
Thunder,
Thunder Cat
HO!

Whisper's World

Whisper Love Summers is who I am. Born free, born alive and born to just be. Even my name sounds free, Whisper...Love...Summers. What was my mother thinking when she gave me this name? Who knows? I guess I will never know. My mother was killed when I was eight-years-old at the hands of her boyfriend, Angelo. I don't remember much. My mother and Angelo always fought. Tears, screams and yelling. Cursing, blood and pain. It's all a blur but momma was buried and Angelo was sent to prison for her death. I ended up living with my Aunt Nora and her three children since my biological father was never in the picture. He left my mother when he found out she was pregnant with me. Well life goes on. That was then, this is now.

Auntie Nora, my mother's only sibling, is a spitting image of my mother. Not just in looks but also when it comes to their taste in men. Auntie Nora had so many men coming in and out of her house when we were little, you would have thought she was trying to create her own army. Auntie Nora was getting her ass beat too by all those fools she labeled as men. I don't know who was worse my mother for getting beat on and killed by one man or my aunt for getting beat on by several men and living to tell the tale. All I know is Whisper Love Summers is not giving her power to any man. As a matter of fact, I'm holding on to my power and I'm getting theirs too. This is my world! I'm fine as hell and that makes my job easier. Let me give you a visual.

I have pretty feet with cute suckable toes that get treated every two to three weeks with a pedicure. Long, lean shapely legs, juicy thighs and a perfectly round ass that's just as bouncy as any one of those chicks in the videos. Do I even need to mention my washboard abs? I guess you get the idea. Long, straight shoulder length

44

black hair. Almond-shaped light brown eyes and soft facial features. Of course all covered in deep, dark chocolate. Now who can ask for a better packaging than that? Seeing my mother and my aunt get slapped around, pushed, kicked and treated like they were nothing, makes me take care of myself. When I feel good and I know I'm looking good, it gives me power and that's where my men come in. My men are different from my Mother's and Auntie Nora's men. Why? The only time my men put their hands on me is to please me.

Now, the man I've been dealing with the longest is Jerome. Jerome is tall at six feet four inches, dark, the blacker the berry the sweeter the juice. Handsome move over Denzel Jerome is in the house. He's forty-five-years old which is exactly twenty years older than me. Jerome owns rental property, a few barbershops, and a clothing store. Jerome not only pays for my two bedroom condominium, but he has furnished it and is the holder of the spare keys to the condo. He gets much respect. Jerome is a hard working businessman who has a full and busy schedule and the woman in his life has to understand that. I do, but too bad his wife doesn't. Shirley, that's her name, gets the hell on my damn nerves. I know she gets on Jerome's nerves too. Always worrying him. Sometimes he's at the condo more than he is at home with her. The two teenage boys are not Jerome's, but children from a previous relationship Shirley was in. Jerome won't divorce her because he's raised those boys like they were his own. He also doesn't want Shirley taking half of everything he's worked for. Shirley knows about me. Hell, Jerome and I have been together for five years and yes she's seen me on numerous occasions. Maybe if she lost weight and grew some damn hair, Jerome would pay some type of attention to her. Jerome still finds time to keep in shape on a regular basis. He jogs, plays basketball, and lifts weights. Jerome always takes care of home, at least my home. Not only did Jerome and I bring in the New Year together, but he bought me a brand new 2007 silver nickel colored Jeep Liberty, fully loaded. He wanted this year to be a smooth ride and that's why I got the SUV. Even though he hasn't been over here in the last two nights, I can still feel the pressure of his body on top of me. The last night he came over he called from his cell phone and all he said was, "Get ready, I'm on my way over." Jerome is a man of few words, but I knew what he meant. Put something sexy on and be prepared to fuck. Since I had already taken a bath when I came in from work earlier, all I needed to do was get out of my sweat-pants, which Jerome hates to see me in, and get out of my wife beater top. I quickly put on an all white, lacey see through, ankle length gown with a plunging v-neck. No panties. I slid my pretty, pedicure feet into my 3 inch heels with the white powder puff on the toes. Threw on some accessories, warm vanilla sugar body oil and fresh-ened my make-up. Just as I finished getting myself to-gether and headed down the stairs, I heard Jerome unlocking the door.

"Hi, baby. How are you?" I asked greeting him at the door with a kiss.

"Better now that I'm here with you."

He gave me the once over, had me spin around to get a rear view and gave a long sigh.

"Looking damn good as usual," he smiled.

"Are you hungry?" I asked him as I headed towards the kitchen. I knew he was watching me as I walked away. I had that sway in my hips that commanded atten-tion.

"I ate earlier, you can grab me a beer though."

He went to the hall closet to hang up his jacket and then disappeared upstairs. I got his beer and poured my-self a glass of white wine. When I got upstairs Jerome was naked, under the covers and watching the sports segment of the news. I gave him his beer and watched as he took a sip then sat the brown bottle next to the lamp on the nightstand. Staying focused on the game of the night, he patted the bed and invited me next to him.

"Come on, baby, get comfortable with me." I took off my slippers and positioned myself in bed. I took a few drinks of my wine and watched Devan Clay hit a three pointer at the last second of the game and bring our local team another win.

"He's the next Michael Jordan, baby," Jerome commented to me.

I was happy to have him here tonight. I was hoping I wouldn't have to sleep alone. He's gotten me use to having him over so much. When Jay Leno started on his monologue that must have been a hint to Jerome to get started on me. He leaned over to my side of the bed, used one hand to play with my hair and his other hand to left my gown up. Before he even came close to my hot spot I was wet. I could hear Jay Leno's audience laughing at a joke Jay told and like the audience, I was feeling joyful too. Jerome begged me to climb on top of him.

"Come on, baby, you know how I like it," he whispered in my ear.

I liked to hear him beg me for it. I waited.

"Whisper, please, I've been thinking of you all day. Feel how hard it is."

He took my hand and placed it on his manhood. He was ready and so was I. I climbed on top of my manly mountain and our bodies entertained each other. He made me hot with every kiss, every lick. I kissed him deeply like I was trying to become a part of him by going through his mouth. I licked his neck down to his nipples that were standing at attention as much as mine were. I let my lips slide down his body to his stiff cock. I slowly took it in my mouth and let my mouth get acquainted with every inch he had. I looked up and saw his eyes rolled to the back of his head. I loved the control I had over him. He was no longer the big man I knew him to be. I broke him down in this way. I licked his shaft up and down and let my tongue tickle the head of his dick non-stop. He moaned and rubbed his hands through my hair. I kept that up until I thought he was going to explode. I wasn't finished with him. I mounted his fat dick and rode it like I was a crazy woman. Pumping up and down. Fast and then slow. Teasing him with the way I glided my hips back and forth. Making him tremble and call my name. It turned me on when he did that. Neither one of us could take it any more and we both came with such an unnatural pressure I was almost knocked off the bed onto the floor. We weren't finished and I knew it. Jerome may have been old school but his sexual appetite was definitely new school. We switched positions with him on top this time and he made love to my body with his tongue. He traveled down to my hot, waiting nest and ate my pussy so damn good it brought tears to my eyes. Jerome once told me Shirley didn't like to give or receive oral sex. She thinks it's nasty. I wish I could tell that stupid bitch it is nasty. Nasty and good. That's why marriages don't work. Wives don't know how to be open-minded enough to not only receive pleasure from their husbands, but to give it as well.

Just when I thought I couldn't take the heat anymore, Jerome flipped me over on my stomach and positioned my ass in the air and drilled my pussy from the back. Biting my pillow, grabbing the sheets, crying out with pleasure, my body tingled with excitement. Damn he was knocking it out! He slapped the back of my ass and I came. I couldn't hold it any longer. He howled like a wild animal caught in a trap in the woods and sprayed his cum all over my ass and back. I felt the warm, thick, milky sweetness of him sliding and dripping from me to the bed. Falling into a heap, catching our breath, he kissed me.

"Damn, Whisper! You sure do know how to treat a man."

We watched some late night movie and fell asleep. I knew my shit was good because Jerome stopped fucking Shirley years ago once he got a whiff of this pussy.

Sometimes when Jerome goes missing in action like he does, that's when I call Bruce. Bruce is Mr. Civil Rights Activist. "As African-American people we need to do this, we need to do that. We not only need our forty-acres and a mule, but in the new millennium we need the house to sit on the forty-acres and a new SUV to sit next to the mule in the driveway." He constantly preached. Bruce was all for Black people and their rights. That's what made him sexy to me. He was our modern day Black Panther. At the age of thirty-seven-years-old, he keeps our city on its toes and keeps the Black community in the know. Even with him being my opposite, he turns me on like a light switch. Bruce is two inches shorter than me at five foot eight. He has a sandy brown complexion with a few freckles across his nose. Reddish brown hair that's low cut and grey eyes. The most exercising he does is when he works the hell out of me. Our last encounter was two weekends ago when he flew out of town to a convention. He called me to tell me he couldn't stand being alone in that big hotel bed and was buying me a ticket to cum, er, I mean to come stay with him. He never takes his wife Charmaine. She hates to fly and doesn't like being left in the hotel room by herself. Either that bitch was just plain stupid or she had another dick on the side. It didn't matter to me, Bruce treats me like a queen when I'm with him. He gives me shopping money whenever we're out of town and we've eaten in so many different restaurants I could become a damn food critic.

Bruce is another freaky bastard. Strange, but I like it. Bruce is what I call a role player. Let's see, I've dressed as a cheerleader, a dominatrix with whips and handcuffs. (There's that power thing again.) I've played a French maid, a belly dancer and even a nun. All roles played in full costume. His favorite character is the hooker. Last time we got together it was off the hook! No pun intended. He picked me up from the airport in Dallas that morning and we went for breakfast. After arriving at the hotel, Bruce showered and got dressed.

"Whisper, I have to get to this seminar. I should be back no later than six o'clock this evening. I'll call if anything changes."

He straightened his tie and put on his suit jacket. I stood in front of him to give him the once over, which he passed. His grey eyes were magnets pulling me in. I grabbed him by his tie and gave him a full passionate kiss.

"Mmmm...I'm so glad you were able to come for the weekend," Bruce said filling both of his hands with my ass.

"I am too. I wanted to give you something to think about while you were in those boring seminars all day." I wiped my lipstick from his mouth with my thumb.

"Baby, you can best believe you'll be on my mind. I already can't wait to get back to you."

"Who knows, I may have a surprise for you when you get back." I gave a sly smile.

"I hope so."

He smiled back and gave me a smack on the ass. After Bruce left I changed clothes, grabbed my swimsuit, and headed to the hotel gym and pool. I worked out and went for a swim. When I got back to the room, I showered, put on some boxers and a t-shirt and ended up falling asleep watching a black and white movie. When I woke up, I realized I had slept longer than I wanted to. It was five-thirty and Bruce would be back to the room shortly. He was always on schedule and I had to rush to get ready and get into character. At exactly six on the dot, I heard the key card being inserted into the door.

"Whisper!" Bruce called out as he set his things down on the dresser.

"Whisper is not here," I said stepping out of the bathroom and leaning against the wall. I was chewing and popping a piece of gum as I watched his reaction. His mouth was open and for a moment it seemed like he was frozen. Finally, he snapped out of his trance and asked,

"Who are you?" He removed his jacket, threw it in a nearby chair and walked towards me.

"Kitty." I answered while still popping my gum.

"Well, Kitty, it's a pleasure to meet you. If you don't mind me asking, why are you in my room?"

His eyes swept over my body as he waited for me to answer.

"I'm here to please you."

I moved closer to him to push him back onto the bed where he fell with no complaints. Standing between his legs I asked, "Do you like what you see?"

"Oh yes."

He rubbed his hands up and down my smooth shaven legs. I was dressed like a trashy whore and he loved it. I was wearing clear stiletto five inch heels, red crotch less panties, a very, very short black mini-skirt, a red tube top with my nipples trying to bust through the material and heavy make-up with strawberry red lipstick. I rubbed my hand across his rock hard rod and asked, "How do you want it?"

"How much are you charging?" he continued with the game.

"This is on me, free of charge." I replied. Taking my gum out and sticking it on the nearby nightstand.

51

"Damn! Well in that case, I want it all. Freaky style."
His face lit up.

"That's the only way I give it."

I immediately got on my knees in front of him, unzipped his pants, whipped out his thick manhood and
wrapped my shiny red lips around his light brown dick
leaving traces of lipstick up and down his shaft. He
moaned with pleasure and lightly held onto my head as it
bobbed up and down on his long, hard pole.

"I'm not ready to cum."

He breathed heavily, stopping my head from moving.
I got up and went to his next favorite position. I got on
my hands and knees, slapped my own ass once and said,
"Come make Kitty purr."

He kicked his shoes off, took off the rest of his clothes,
got behind me and entered my pussy doing it doggie
style. I knew it was good by the way he was grunting
and calling my name. Once again I broke him down. We
talked dirty which I know we both love. There was hair
grabbing, ass slapping, sweat dripping and plenty of
cummin'. Our worlds were rocked and we were both satisfied. After ordering room service and getting our grub
on, we did it all over again. This time I had to let him
know I was the one who ran this show. I went straight
for the dick with a mission. I sucked his dick like I was
sucking on a thick milkshake through a little ass straw. I
loved the sweet taste of his juices. His dick was smooth
and I loved how it filled my mouth. It brought me more
pleasure to see how he twitched and moaned. Damn, he
was like a little bitch. He howled and I kept sucking like I
didn't hear him. I played with his balls and I think that's
what brought him to the brink. He grabbed me by my
hair and came in my mouth. I felt the warm flow glide
down the back of my neck. Bruce was trembling and
whimpering like a baby. I had even came a little just off
his reaction. It was thrilling for me to feel like I had him

not only in my mouth, but in the palms my hands too.

The next morning I awoke to six one-hundred dollar bills on the night stand with a note that read:

Thank you, Kitty, for last night, it was wonderful.
I left the car for you to go shopping.
I hope this is enough. See you for dinner.
Bruce

I had a great time shopping and the rest of the weekend was very climaxing for the both of us. Once again I had to do things Mrs. Wifey won't do. Mission complete.

Finally, there's Devan Clay. He's a twenty-one-year-old professional basketball player. His high school sweetheart got pregnant on purpose once she found out he was going to the pros right after high school graduation. After the graduation, after the signing, after the baby, they got married. Smart girl, she doesn't have to work and she is married to not only the hottest but one of the highest paid athletes in the NBA. Problem is, Nicole, her family and her friends are straight ghetto. He says he's tired of the "gold teeth wearing, weed smoking, no job having bastards" at his new house all day. Devan wants someone more mature as well as someone who isn't afraid to explore sexually. That's where I come in. Devan and I met a year ago while I was shopping in the mall. We've been kicking it ever since. To get away from Nicole, Devan has a condo on the other side of town where we meet for our fun. Devan is completely hooked on me licking his ass then letting him straight fuck me in mine. He also loves when I masturbate for him. A night with Devan begins pretty normal like any other couple. He sometimes cooks for us or we do take out. We watch movies or play his favorite game on X-Box which he al-

53

ways beats me. He'll talk to me about his problems with Nicole sometimes too. She's lazy, never cleans, always has a house full of people when he's traveling and if it wasn't for his son, he would have left a long time ago. Blah, blah, blah. I've heard this story a million times. After all of that, the night ends on a kinky note. I start out masturbating for him. Sometimes I do it with a vibrator or a dildo and sometimes I use my fingers. Rule is I have to do it until I reach my first climax then it becomes all about him and me. Devan gets straight to the point. He flips me over on my stomach and lubricates what some may call the Forbidden City, and then he gets deep into it. His toffee colored six foot seven inch frame humps the shit out of my black ass. Once again, no pun intended.

"Whisper, this feels so fucking good." He says between heavy moans as he bangs my ass over and over. The only response I can give is a moan here, a grunt there and little screams in between. I have to admit, he gets the best of me in this position. Just as I think I'm about to split permanently in half, he cums like an unexpected storm on a clear day. Getting us both tall glasses of fresh fruit juice, (Devan doesn't drink alcohol) we watch television for awhile and then it's my turn to stun his mind. I have him lay on his stomach and I spread his cheeks so I can slide my warm, wet tongue back and forth. I get him so excited he buries his face deep in the pillows and he cries out like a bitch. My tongue explores his hole and I know it brings him great pleasure because he grips the sheets like he's falling off a cliff and is trying to hang on for dear life. He gives a loud growl and cums hard.

"How are you doing?" I ask coming up to lay beside him.

"Real good," he replies giving me a kiss and wrapping his arms around me.

As he falls asleep next to me, I think of how lucky

Nicole is to have a husband who wants to be a family man, and at such a young age. Acting the way she does he'll never be one with her. He's a really sweet guy. So he's a little kinky, what man isn't? The next morning we sex each other up and down before we part, going our separate ways.

Like I said I haven't seen Jerome in two days and it's been two weeks since Bruce and I spent time together. Now that I think about it, Devan has been preparing for the playoffs, so it will be awhile before I get to spend any real time with him. They've all sent little gifts, flowers, lingerie, and jewelry. Their way of saying they miss me.

"I guess I'll enjoy this time to myself." I reach for a book I've wanted to read and before I could get into the first chapter good, my phone rings. I wonder who it could be as I take the receiver off the base. I look at the caller ID and the name doesn't appear, only "UNKNOWN CALLER." Jerome, Bruce and Devan all have private numbers that don't show up on the caller ID screen. "Who needs to spend time in my world?" I asked out loud as I pushed the talk button on the phone.

"Hello?"

"Whisper, I've been missing you."

Time for me to pull out my bag of tricks and prove who's really in control.

Imagination

I imagine you and I embracing in a passionate kiss
Your warm tongue anxiously searching for mine
You find it

I imagine you slowly removing my clothes and discover-
ing
The real secret Victoria has been hiding

I imagine it being my turn as I slowly remove your
clothes
I try to keep calm, the excitement is building
I want this moment to last
And last it does

My mouth and my tongue explore your body
Like its new found land discovered by foreign travelers
Welcome home

I imagine us taking our time
Since for this moment time is all we have
During this time I make love to you
Not fuck you like a lover normally would

I imagine you're an ice cream cone stacked high and cold
on a hot summer day
I gently lick your ear
You have two so I do it twice
I lick your neck ever so lightly
I feel chill bumps lace your body
I lick, suck and kiss your nipples
Give them the special attention they desire
Usually forgotten
I run my tongue down the middle of your strong chest
until I reach your belly button

Where I let my tongue get dizzy going around, around
and around again
I hear you take in a deep breath and hold it
You know what's next
That will have to wait, I'm not going to do what you ex-
pect
At least not now

I imagine you more in control and taking over the situa-
tion
You turn me on my back
You smother my body in sweet, long kisses
You take my breasts in your mouth
As your hands become familiar with the rest of who I am
I feel scorching and burning because the heat is rising

First degree
Second degree
Third degree burns

I imagine my legs slowly being parted and lifted by your
masculine hands
Legs being lifted and placed on broad shoulders
The same shoulders that normally holds the weight of the
world on them

I imagine you not being able to hold on to self control
Please
Let go
Self control gone

I imagine the in and out motion of our personal spaces
invading one another
Our lips, our tongues meeting like it's their last time

I imagine sweat dripping `

Sheet grabbing
Pillow biting
Back straining
Ass slapping
Deep throat moaning
Hair pulling
Shoulder biting
Name calling
Deep concentration thinking on how a piece of heaven
landed here on earth

Then I imagine us climbing to the highest mountain
The air so different it makes our heads light
Standing at the top of that mountain
Breathing hard, breathing heavy
Just standing on that peak
Having reached that peak and letting out screams
Screams of passion

That's what I imagine

Getting High

I'm getting high
High off of you and the things you do
I inhale your sweetness
Let it fill my insides
Feel it tingle throughout my body and settle into my
bloodstream

When I exhale I'm letting out the stress of your day
Your worries
Your fears
I exhale all of your pain

I slowly take another puff and continue to taste you on
my lips
I inhale your strength and all your manly ways
With you on my tongue
I sit back and close my eyes
I'm just sitting here getting high

Getting high off of you

Unconditional Love

Tiffany and I have been best friends for what seems like eternity. She was the new girl on our block one Summer when her family moved into the house across the street from ours. I was always sitting on the porch watching the other children play. Sometimes I'd read a book or just daydream on the porch swing. I didn't feel comfortable playing with the children in the neighborhood so I kept to myself. One day the new girl who I had been watching play and get to know everyone on the block came out of her house and marched right across the street to our gate.

"How come you don't ever come off the porch?" She just came right out and asked.

"I don't like them too much," I replied looking in the direction of the other kids. "They don't like me either." I looked down at my shoes.

"Who cares?" she asked coming inside the gate and up the steps. "They are so stupid anyway." She frowned up her face and sat next to me on the swing. "Want some?" She took a beat up brown paper bag out of her pocket. It was filled with different candies. She had Now and Laters, Mary Janes, jawbreakers, Chick-O-Sticks, sunflower seeds and wine candy. "Yeah!" I exclaimed excitedly. We sat on the porch for the rest of the afternoon eating candy, talking and enjoying each other's company. From that time forward Tiffany and I have had a special friendship, a special bond. She always accepted me for who I was even though a lot of other people didn't. She always made me feel strong and confident and we would do anything for each other.

Just as I was walking in the house the phone rang. I threw my bags down and ran to my bedroom to get it.

"Hello," I answered.

60

"Where have you been all day?" Tiffany asked.

"Hey, girl," I said kicking off my high heel sandals and laying across the bed. "I had to go get my hair done. Foxy Blue laid me out." I looked in the dresser mirror at my hair. Foxy Blue was my hairstylist and the best stylist in the city. She had a chic salon on the north side of town called Blue's Groove. Baby, it was the place to go for everything, massages, facials, pedicures, manicures, body wraps and many other pampering services.

"I know Foxy hooked you up 'cause she ain't gonna let you nobody walk out looking crazy." Tiff stated. "I need to call her myself and make an appointment for later in the week."

"Yeah you do with the ping, ping, pings you got going on with the back of your neck," I said playfully.

"Shut up! It ain't that bad," Tiff laughed.

"So what's up with you?" I asked.

"Nothing. I got up and cleaned my house and I need to run some errands. You performing tonight?"

I have a part time job singing at a club called the Golden Showers. It is a nice club, always packed, especially on the weekends. I make pretty good money for it to be just a hobby. My real job is being a make-up artist and stylist for a local soap opera, Every Life.

"Yeah, I'm doing the 11:30 show. You should come down. You haven't seen me perform in awhile and I miss hearing you scream out for me in the audience."

"I know," she said sadly. "It's just..."

"You don't even have to explain." I interrupted. "I already know. I just don't want you sitting up in that house like you're ninety years old." I felt so sorry for Tiff. She had everything she wanted and needed. Her boyfriend Rico made sure of that. The condo she lives in Rico bought for her as a birthday present. The SUV she drives was a Christmas present from him as well. Not to mention all the jewelry and clothes. She always kept her job as a manager at the department store because even though Rico and his dope dealing weren't legit, she wanted to be. Rico's been locked up for a year and a half now and Tiff still hurts like it was yesterday when he was sentenced.

"I'm coming to see you tonight," she said trying to sound more upbeat. "You better perform your ass off."

"All right." I cheered excitedly.

"Well, I better finish doing what I have to do if I'm going out tonight."

"I'll see you when you get to the club."

"If it's okay with you, I'm going to follow you home and stay over at your place."

"Tiff, that's no problem at all. You know I love having you over."

"Thanks. I don't feel like staying by myself tonight. I'll see you later." We hung up and I turned on the television then decided to take a nap to be well rested for my performance.

"Koffie you blew the roof off of Golden Showers tonight. When you did Jennifer Holliday's song *Husband*, I was blown away. When you ended with Patti LaBelle's version of *Somewhere over the Rainbow*, I was too through with you. You were jammin'."

"Thank you, thank you. And speaking of jamming, I saw you after the show getting your groove thang on with Elliot," I said jokingly.

"Elliot is fine with those pretty, light brown eyes and he's too fine to be gay. " She said throwing a bag of popcorn in the microwave.

"I've got to wash all of this make-up off. Bring me some Sprite when you come to my room."

After I washed my face and slipped on my pajamas, I met Tiff in my room. She had found an old shirt of mine to sleep in and was lying across the bed with the bowl of popcorn watching Halle Berry in BAPS for the one-hundredth time.

"This was the only decent thing on television," she said handing the bowl of popcorn to me. "Thanks for letting me stay the night. I didn't feel like being alone."

"Girl, you know I don't care. I'm glad you're here, I never get to see you anymore." We sat in silence for a minute watching Halle dancing while waiting to get into the audition, when Tiff finally spoke.

"I talked to Rico yesterday."

"How is he doing?" I asked.

"As well as can be expected. I drive down to see him next week. I can't wait until his time is up." She stared at the movie like she couldn't afford to miss a scene.

"Just hang in there, his time will be up before you know it." I got comfortable under the covers.

"I hope so. By the way, he has a buddy that wants to write to one of my girlfriends. How about it?"

"He said one of your girlfriends." I laughed.

"You are my best girlfriend." She playfully slapped my arm.

"Ple-ee-se." I said smacking my lips. "What about Crystal, Zamia, or Tammy?"

"Okay, where do I start? Crystal is too lazy to go anywhere or do anything. Zamia only calls when she needs something and Tammy is faker than a three dollar bill with a picture of Malcolm X on the front."

"Now that's fake," I said laughing and shoved popcorn in my mouth.

"Here!" she said reaching for her purse. "I have his name and information right here."

"I don't want that." I protested and pushed the paper back into her hand.

"Come on, take it. You haven't talked to anybody since Kevin." She forced the paper back into my hand.

"You just had to bring that up. You can't let sleeping

dogs lie, can you?"

"That's exactly what he was, a dog," she replied sharply.

I thought Kevin was "the one." He was 6'3", handsome, muscular and treated me like the queen I am. He was the owner of a small computer programming company, which he started after he was injured during his rookie year playing professional football. At that time, I was a cosmetic consultant at the same department store where Tiffany is now a manager. Since the store didn't open until 10 o'clock, I didn't have to be there until a few minutes before the doors opened for business. Sometimes Kevin would stop by my place before he went to the office. He had a little joke when I'd open the door. "I already ate breakfast, but I came all the way across town to get some Koffie." That would always make me laugh. Kevin knew me well, inside and out and I thought I knew him just as well.

One day I was at work when a customer came to my counter stating she wanted to try a make over for a big event that was coming up. "Nothing too bold, soft and natural is what I'm looking for." She told me.
"No problem." I replied. I invited her to sit in my chair at the counter and we got down to business. I asked her questions about the make-up she normally wore, what she cleaned her face with, if she had any problems with her skin and began to clean her face and get out the supplies I would need. Whenever I did a make over, I would take two before photos and two after photos. One set would go to the customer and the other set would go into my files. She was a really down to earth person and we were having a good conversation until I asked her what was the occasion she was getting all dolled up for.
"My wedding. Let me show you pictures of my fiancé and our 3-years-old daughter." She went into her purse

and pulled out a mini photo album, which she handed to me. I flipped it open and the first picture I saw was a cute little chocolate drop girl playing with a pail and shovel in the sand. She had the two biggest afro puffs I'd seen in a long time. I had to laugh. "She is too cute with all that hair." I told my customer.

"Don't let the cuteness fool you. She is a handful and my fiancé wants to have another baby."

I turned to the next page and there he was, holding my customer in his arms with the bluest wide body of water and the bluest skies for the background. I almost fell out but I had to keep my composure.

"What's his name?" I asked like I didn't know.

"Kevin," she said smiling. "He's my dream come true."

My mind began to churn and I didn't know what to say or do. I had to keep it together. I wanted to know everything. I had to know everything. How could Kevin do this to me? Ignorant bastard!

"So where were the pictures taken?" I continued flipping through the photo album.

"We went to the Bahamas this past winter."

This past winter? It was probably the time Kevin was gone for a week and had told me he had to go to Florida to check out a new business venture.

"That's nice. The Bahamas, how long did you stay?"

"A week and I loved every minute of its" she smiled.

"How long have you two known each other?"

"We've known each other for five years, but we just got engaged a year ago. I didn't ever think we'd get married. It seems like it took him forever to ask."

Silently I remained in shock as I listened to her talk about Kevin. I thought to myself again, how could he do this to me? A wave of nausea came over me. Then I thought to myself, how could he do this to this woman and this precious child? What kind of man was I dating?

65

I finished her make over and she loved it.

"Oh my goodness, this is perfect," she said excitedly.

"You were easy to work with." I stated still trying to hold myself together. I ended the make over session with her, rung up her purchases and gave her the two photos.

"Do you have any business cards? I'd like to give them to my bridal party. Maybe we can hire you to do all of our make-up the day of the wedding."

"Sure let me get you some." I went to my cabinet and got out some cards for her. "Call me if you'd like to set up a time for you and your bridal party."

When she left, I took the rest of the day off. I felt too sick to work the rest of my shift. Later that night when Kevin came over, I showed him the two snapshots of his fiancée I had taken.

"What kind of relationship do you think I could have with you?" he asked me. "I know you weren't serious about this." He said with an attitude.

I cursed him to hell and kicked him out of my apartment. I was a wreck for the rest of the week. I found out through his fiancée where the wedding was going to be held and I decided to be the make-up artist for her and her party, plus attend the wedding. I had to see for myself if Kevin was really going to go through with this wedding. I watched the ceremony from the back of the church. My heart was full of pain when they both said "I do." When it was time to greet the couple as husband and wife, I walked up and shook Kevin's hand. He looked like he had seen a ghost. "Congratulations!" I said and walked off. I ended up taking two weeks off from work going through a depression. Do you know that fool tried to come over after getting back from his honeymoon? I couldn't believe it. To be honest, even after what he did, I never got over him, but I wasn't stupid enough to continue playing his fool either.

"Just write to him. How bad can it be? We're not talking marriage. We're talking about a pen pal for goodness sake," Tiff was saying breaking my train of thought. She rolled her eyes and shook her head. I didn't even look at the slip of paper, I just took it and put it on my nightstand next to the digital clock and finished watching the movie.

Two weeks later I got my mail out of the mailbox and headed to the kitchen like I normally do, that way, I can throw away junk mail immediately and not have it around my house. "Trash, trash, trash." I said aloud as I pitched unwanted advertisements and coupons in the garbage can. "Whoa! Who wrote to me?" I asked myself looking at the plain white envelope. I didn't recognize the handwriting, but it was definitely addressed to me. Koffie Hamilton, 1602 Water Crest Way. I looked in the upper left hand corner to see who it was from. A Mr. Perry St. James, State Prison Correctional Center. "Prison!" I shouted. "Who in the hell?" I immediately opened the envelope.

> **Dear Koffie,**
> **I received your letter yesterday and was very excited to hear from you.**
> "What letter?" I asked myself.
> **I didn't expect to hear from anyone but Rico's girl friend Tiffany told me she had a very close friend who may be interested.**

I'm going to kill Tiffany. What has that girl gone off and done? I raced to my bedroom because I remembered that slip of paper by the clock Tiff had given to me the night she stayed over. Sure enough, the same name on the paper matched the name on the envelope. I dialed Tiff's number. Her voicemail came on so I left a message.

"Tiffany, I am going to get you. I received a letter today from a Mr. Perry St. James stating he received a letter from me. You wouldn't happen to know anything about that would you? Give me a call as soon as you get this message. Bye." I then lay across my bed and because my curiosity got the best of me, I finished reading the letter. By the end of the letter, I knew quite a bit about Mr. St. James. He was 35-years old, had an 11-year-old daughter named Kiara and he was working towards a degree in hopes of becoming a youth counselor upon his release. He said he wanted to work with young boys because he didn't want to see them take the same path he took and end up in prison. He was in for selling drugs and he wanted out of that lifestyle. He described himself as 6"5', 220 pounds, muscular build, brown eyes, black short hair and a medium complexion. I must admit, he sounded very attractive. I had finished the letter when the phone rang.

"Koffie, don't be angry. I typed a letter to Perry and told him a little about you because I didn't think you would and I've talked to him before through Rico and he sounds real nice, not to mention cute and you know Rico don't hang with just anybody and if Rico likes him you know he has to be cool." Tiff was talking non stop.

"All right, all right," I said laughing and cutting her off from her rambling marathon. "Stop and catch your breath." I couldn't help but laugh.

"I just thought it would be nice for you to write to him, you know, get to know each other as friends and if anything happens from it, let it flow."

"You know how I feel about leaving people in the dark," I reminded her.

"Look," she said assuring me, "everything is going as planned. Let it flow."

She was right, she's never steered me wrong before. We continued talking about Perry and all she knew about him. She also told me what information she put in the letter so when I wrote back to him I wouldn't be repeating myself. At the end of the conversation I promised her I would write back to him and keep her posted. This was going to be very interesting. And honestly, I was looking forward to seeing how this was going to turn out.

It's been three months since Perry and I have started writing to one another. I receive letters from him twice a week, sometimes three times a week. He definitely gets just as many cards and letters from me too. I've found out so much about him, from his favorite foods and books to what type of person he used to be and what type of person he's trying to become. He learned everything about me as too. Well, almost everything. I just didn't know how to tell him about certain parts of my past or when to tell him. Writing about it in a letter seems so impersonal. What difference does it really make? He wasn't getting out for another two years anyway. I'll have things more in place by then. If we last that long. I guess.

"Koffie, are you sure you haven't heard anything?"

"I'm positive, Lynn, absolutely nothing." Lynn plays Nikki Blaine on Every Life and Lynn was worried her character was getting the ax. Nikki Blaine is the fiancée of Dex Criss, the wealthiest man in Mason Bay. Dex's former lover, Diane Wills is back in town and wants her man. Two days ago she ran Nikki Blaine off of the road. Diane has told Dex she'll do anything to stop the wedding of him and Nikki from taking place. Dex is now torn between Nikki and Diane, but what no one knows is that Diane and Dex are half brother and sister. Instead of Lynn wearing her flawless make-up as the high fashion model, Nikki, Lynn is the touch and go-barely-hanging-on, hospital gown wearing Nikki. "No one has said anything about me?"

"Honey, the only thing everyone is talking about is how high our ratings are and the possibility of being moved to a national television station at prime time. It would be like Dallas or Dynasty back in the day." I laughed out loud at the thought of it all.

"Koffie, let me know if you hear anything, okay?"

"I promise. Now stop worrying and let's get you finished up for this next scene."

"Thanks."

She gave me a quick hug and I finished applying the heavy make-up to her left eye to give it a bruised look. When I finished, she rushed off to the set. I cleaned my work area and put away my products and settled in my director's chair to read my most recent letter from Perry. He wrote a poem saying our love is like a flower in the spring beginning to bloom. It was so sweet and romantic. It made me wonder what my life could be like with him in it.

Fall had come and gone and Winter was here. Perry and I continued to keep in contact on a regular basis. With Christmas right around the corner, I mailed Perry one Christmas card with a different theme for a week. I also put some money on his books hoping it would be enough to last at least a month. The biggest thing I did was sending him my phone number. We have never talked over the phone and I was nervous about doing so. I sent the number in enough time for him to get it right at Christmas.

"Girl, he sounds so sexy," Tiff was telling me again. "I can't believe you held out this long not giving him your number."

She was helping me hang lights and decorate the house.

"I just wanted to get to know him through the letters we sent first. What would I have done with a high phone bill and a man I didn't like?" I moved across the living room to replay the Nat King Cole CD again.

"Yes, I guess you're right," she changed the subject.

"You sure you won't change your mind about coming home for the holidays? It will only be a few days."

"I'm sure, Tiffany. You know how my family feels about my situation."

"That was so long ago. I'm quite sure they've changed by now. You need to contact them." She said trying to convince me.

"That may seem like a long time to you, but baby, it seems just like yesterday to me." I snapped. "The whole house went crazy that day. You would have thought I told them I killed the president of the United States. Look, forget it. I don't want to ruin this happy moment. Please can we talk about something else?"

"You'll never know unless you communicate. You got some popcorn?" she quickly asked and headed towards the kitchen.

"You know where I keep it," I answered and continued decorating. I hope she understood how I felt and what I said about my family. Who knows, maybe one day I will contact them.

On Christmas morning when I woke up, the first thing I did was look out of the window. The snow blanketed the neighborhood. All the cars, trees, rooftops and in front of some doors the snow had drifted high and deep. The streets were quiet and pretty but I bet inside of those homes it was total Christmas chaos. I had performed last night at Golden Shower and the place was packed. I had a great time. People were wishing each other happy holidays and exchanging gifts and cards. There was plenty of food for everyone and it was wonderful seeing everyone enjoy themselves. I loved this time of year. After taking a bath and putting on a new red satin lounge pajama set, I headed to the kitchen to fix me a nice breakfast. I cooked buttery grits, fluffy scrambled eggs, nicely browned toast, tasty sausage links and had a cold glass of

71

orange juice. I decided to eat in the living room with all of the Christmas lights and watch some television. The movie, "It's a Wonderful Life" was just coming on. That had to be my all time favorite Christmas movie. I could-n't even count the number of times I've seen it. I was half way through my breakfast when the phone rang. I picked up the cordless phone next to me, "Merry Christ-mas." I chimed.

"I knew you'd be up!" Tiff screamed into the phone.

"You're my girl!"

"You must have opened your gift from me." I was laughing knowing that had to be it.

"You know I did. Thank you, thank you, thank you!" she was laughing and shouting.

I purchased four different fragrances from Victoria's Secret. The bath and shower gel, the lotion, plus the body spray. I also gave her four lingerie sets and a fifty dollar gift certificate.

"That really isn't your gift," I stated. "I had Rico in mind when I was buying all of that."

She fell out laughing.

"Trust me, we will both enjoy it when he gets home."

We stayed on the phone for awhile with her telling me who she saw from the old neighborhood and school. She was dishing out all the gossip and I was cracking up. Af-ter we finished talking, it seemed like my phone turned into the hot line. Call after call of friends and co-workers poured in. Everyone was calling to wish me a Merry Christmas or to invite me to a Christmas dinner. By 4:30 I had talked to everybody. I had even talked to friends who I hadn't heard from since last Christmas. I was cleaning up the kitchen and finishing up my small dinner when the phone rang again. "Hello and Merry Christ-mas." I answered joyfully. An automated voice then spoke,

You have a collect call from an inmate at Central State

Prison. Caller state your name.

"Perry."

I had forgotten I had sent Perry my home number.

Will you accept the call? Press one if yes, or press two if no.

I nervously pressed one on the dial pad.

"Merry Christmas, Koffie." His deep voice sounded smooth and soothing.

"Merry Christmas, Mr. St. James. It's a pleasure to hear your voice," I smiled.

"Yours as well. I would have called first thing this morning, but everyone here was trying to call family and all of the phones were crowded."

"I understand. I'm glad you were able to get through."

"Thanks, Koffie, for the cards. I have all of them hanging on my locker. That's as close as I'll get to Christmas decorations this year. And you didn't have to send the money. I'm not out to break anybody or take anything, especially from a woman."

"Perry, you didn't break me or take from me. It's a Christmas gift and I didn't mind at all. I'm glad I had it to send and I hope it was enough."

"It was plenty and once again thank you."

We picked up our conversation from where we last left off in a letter. He sounded just as sweet and down to earth as he did in those letters. I had sent him a few scripts of "Every Life" so he would know what was going on with the characters on the soap opera. As I was giving him the update about Shelly being pregnant with her husband's twin brother's baby, an automated voice cut in,

You have one minute remaining on this call.

"Well that was quick." I said.

"I can already tell there will never be enough time to talk to you."

"Perry, you are so sweet."

"If it's okay with you, I would like to call you again,"

"That would be great. Sunday mornings are best for

73

me. We can make it every Sunday."

"You've got yourself a date," he laughed. At that point, we ended our conversation and I sat back on the couch and smiled. "That deserves a cup of eggnog." I said aloud and headed for the kitchen.

I met Tiff at her place the day she got back in town and she was bearing more gifts for me from people back home.

"Everybody misses you and wants to see you again."

"I bet they do." I said rolling my eyes. Tiff began putting all of her things away and showing me her gifts as I opened mine. We talked about everybody and everything.

"I can't believe Roselyn has six children now." I commented.

"Maybe that's why she was voted most popular girl in high school." Tiff said and we both screamed with laughter.

"Girl, you're crazy." I said wiping tears from my eyes.

"Guess who I talked to?" I asked.

"Who?"

"Perry."

Her eyes got wide. "When? Why are you just now telling me? What did he say? Doesn't he sound sexy?" She was asking a million questions at once.

"Slow your roll," I said putting my hand up like it was a stop sign. "We spoke on Christmas and I wanted to wait until you got back home before I said anything. We didn't talk long, you know how the phones time you and yes he sounds very sexy."

"Y'all gonna talk again?"

"We decided every Sunday morning." I said smiling. She squealed. "I knew it would work out."

"Well, we'll see." I replied.

New Year's had come and gone. Tiff and I had brought in the New Year at her house in our pajamas watching the never aging Dick Clark. At midnight, people in her neighborhood let off fireworks. It was so pretty.

On Sunday mornings I would get up, get myself together and fix breakfast. By that time, Perry's call would come in and we'd begin our breakfast date. All week long I would look forward to his calls. If he was late, he'd say, "Everybody beat me to the phone this morning." I'd be okay after that. Our time over the phone had become special and intimate. We got to know so much more about one another. I felt like I knew him all of my life. I just wish I could tell him about what was happening with me.

"Koffie, I wouldn't even worry about that. Everything will be taken care of soon and you will be able to live normal and not have that burden on your shoulders."

"I guess you're right," I still sounded unsure and worried.

"What do I always tell you? Let it flow. It's going to be alright. You and Perry get along great and he loves you for the person you are. When he meets you, what's not to love?"

"Tiff, you've always helped me to see the brighter side of things. Spring is right around the corner, I'll have my surgery and I'll be blooming like wild flowers in a field." I began to feel better. "Let's go to the video store and get some movies." I suggested.

"How about we pick up some Chinese food on the way back? I'm starved."

"As much as you've been eating, if Rico wasn't locked up I'd swear you were pregnant."

"Whatever!" she laughed.

I began to think of how much I couldn't wait for

Spring to arrive.

Perry and I were getting closer as time passed. We exchanged photos, he wrote poems and drew wonderful artwork. I mailed him scripts from the show, newspaper articles, cards and every once in awhile, put some money on his books. We always had great conversations and we learned and taught each other so much. He mentioned marriage on one of our dates.

"Have you thought about getting married one day?"

"That's a girl's favorite dream." I replied.

"Have you ever thought about us getting married?" he asked.

"Mr. St. James, I cannot tell a lie," I smiled. "Of course I have."

"I have too. Maybe we can talk about it more in the future and make plans for a wedding."

"That would be nice," I said softly.

Later I was telling Tiff about the conversation I had with Perry.

"He is so sweet. I can't believe it."

"I knew you two would get along. That's just what you needed especially since that damn Kevin."

"Kevin who?" I asked like I didn't know who she was talking about.

"That's right, forget all about him. Now aren't you glad I mailed that letter to Perry?"

"You're my girl. You're constantly looking out for me. Speaking of looking out for me, you're still going to the hospital with me, right?" I asked in a serious tone.

"Wild horses couldn't keep me away. I've already arranged my days off at work, so we're all set for the big day."

I was relieved to hear that. I don't think I could go through this without Tiff. She was my rock in my tough situations.

76

"You remember Erica Hopson?" she asked. "The clerk who took your place in the cosmetic department after you left?" She reminded me.

"How could I forget her dingy butt? She had it all downstairs and nothing upstairs, if you know what I mean."

"I know exactly what you mean. Anyway, she had her breasts enlarged by Dr. Horowitz, the same doctor who is operating on you."

"Well it looks like ol' doc did a good job. I think it's a little too much for someone as small as she is, but obviously she's happy," I said.

"You know she has the nerve to call them Pleasure and Heaven?"

"You are lying!" I shouted.

We had to take time to laugh at that one. After the laughter died down I informed her I had told Perry I was going into the hospital.

"Really? What did he say?"

"I just told him I was going in for some much needed surgery I had put off for too long and I would discuss it with him at a later time."

"Good idea."

"He respected my privacy and left it as that."

"Koffie, take it one day at a time and you should be fine."

"I'm planning on it. So, how's Rico? Perry said he was moved to another dorm area to make room for some new inmates."

"Yes, he was moved to another unit last week. He's doing okay. Neither one of us can wait until he gets home."

"Thank goodness he doesn't have that much longer," I told her.

"Koffie I'm really going to miss you while you're recovering from your surgery."

Lynn a.k.a. Nikki Blaine was telling me. "I'm going to miss you too. Just make sure you call and keep me posted on all the gossip that's going on around here. I'm not talking about the show either. I'm talking about behind the scenes."

"In that case, I'll be talking to you so much it'll be like you never left." Laughing, I finished brushing up her long blonde hair in a French roll. I had already done her make up, so all she had to do was go to wardrobe and get into the floor length blue sequin tight fitting evening gown they selected for the next scene. The next scene was a party at Mason Bay's City Hall. Even though Nikki Blaine won the heart of Dex Criss and they were married now, Nikki was having an affair with Mayor Tim Goldman.

"Have you seen the gown I'm wearing?"

"Yes, girl. You are going to be fierce. I did you up to have a more elegant look, plus the way I did your eyes is going to bring out the blue in them more and will look perfect with that blue gown. You are going to be a knockout."

"I'm glad I've been eating right and working out. That gown is so tight I can hardly breathe. I hope I won't have to be in it too long. It's beautiful but uncomfortable."

"You'll do fine." I smiled at her through the mirror.

"There, all done." I sprayed her hair with a holding spray.

"Great job as always, Koffie." She began to dig into her duffel bag. "If you need anything while you're off let me know."

She pulled out a medium size white square box with a pink ribbon around it. Handing the box to me she said, "This is a small hurry-up-and-get-well gift."

"Oh, Lynn." I whispered in shock as I reached for the box. "You didn't have to get me anything. It's not like

I'm leaving forever."

"Eight weeks is too long for me," she said with tears in her eyes. "You're going to make me cry and mess up my beautiful make-up job you did. Don't open it now, I'll start blubbering. Wait until I leave."

"Thank you Lynn." I hugged her tight.

"I hope your replacement doesn't have me looking like a clown. I met her yesterday and she seems like such a bitch."

I covered my mouth and laughed. "She's good. I picked her myself."

"No one is as good as you," Lynn said.

She gathered her things and left. I sat in my director's chair and took the pink ribbon off first. I then lifted the lid to find a silver link necklace with a gorgeous rose quartz stone dangling from the bottom. It is said the rose quartz is a woman's stone giving her energy and inner strength. I loved it and immediately put it on. Later that day the rest of the crew surprised me with lunch, balloons, flowers, teddy bears and candy. My last day before my medical leave was wonderful. On my drive home from the studio, I already began to miss everyone.

The night before my surgery, Tiff stayed over at my place so she could drive me to the hospital early that morning. Perry also made a surprise call.

"Hey, baby." He said in that deep, sexy voice. "I was thinking about you and wanted to tell you good luck with the surgery."

"Thank you, baby."

My smile stretched from ear to ear. I told him about what my co-workers had done for me on my last day of work and let him know that Tiff was going to be taking care of me.

"Right now I'm more excited than nervous, I think."

"You'll be fine. I sent some prayers up for you. I'm

also glad to know Tiffany is there for you. I wish I could be. Look, I know this isn't one of our regular scheduled calls, so I'm not going to keep you long. I know you have to get up early in the morning, so get your rest and I'll talk to you later."

"Thanks for calling. You know when I get back so call me then."

"I will. Sweet dreams."

"Bye. I love you."

"I love you too."

Tiff and I sat up for another hour talking like always and flicking through the channels. Then we both decided to go to sleep. Tomorrow is finally here and I can't wait. My life will be complete.

"Are you nervous?" Tiff asked.

"A little." I checked in with admissions and signed the necessary forms. I was given directions on where to go to begin what would be the rest of my life. I changed into the infamous open back gown the nurse had given me and was propped on a gurney. Tiff had all of my personal items sitting next to her in my overnight bag. The nurse stepped in, "Ms. Hamilton, the doctor will be in shortly to go over the procedure with you and answer any last minute questions you may have."

"Thank you." I said nervously and the nurse left.

"Quick, let me have your hands."

Tiff reached out for my hands as she jumped out of her seat.

"Let's pray," she said.

With our eyes closed, heads bowed and holding hands, Tiff said a prayer asking God to be with me and the doctors through this surgery and she prayed for a successful operation and a quick recovery. "Amen." We said in unison. Just then Dr. Horowitz came in.

"Good morning," he said cheerfully.

His upbeat attitude made me feel more relaxed. I introduced him to Tiffany and he then went on to explain what would take place during the operation and the recovery period.

"Don't worry, Ms. Hamilton, you and your friend will not have to memorize all of these instructions. I'll have one of my nurses give you a sheet with all of the information on it." He smiled and asked, "Any questions?"

He looked at me to Tiff and back to me again.

"No. No questions," I answered.

"Well then," he clapped his hands together, "as Arsenio Hall used to say, let's get busy." He chuckled.

"I'll see you in the recovery room." Tiff leaned in to hug me.

Sometime later I was trying to get my thoughts together when I heard,

"Koffie, are you okay?"

I couldn't talk like I normally do and I tried to clear my throat as best as I could. Tiff saw that I was having trouble and reached for a Styrofoam cup filled with ice water and a straw. She put the straw to my lips and allowed me to take a few sips. In my loudest whisper I shouted, "I did it!" She squeezed my hand and smiled.

"Yes, you did it. Get some rest and the doctor will be in later to check on you."

I nodded in agreement. Apparently I must have fallen asleep immediately because I heard someone trying to wake me up. I opened my eyes to see a white middle aged nurse standing over me smiling.

"I have to get up so soon?" I asked in a much clearer voice than the last time I spoke.

"Sweetie, you've been asleep for two hours."

"Two hours?" I repeated. "Where's Tiffany?"

"Oh, your friend? She went down to the cafeteria about twenty minutes ago. How are you feeling, honey?"

"A little groggy."

"Any pain?"

"Yes. A little. More like an uncomfortable feeling."

"I'll get you something for that. The doctor will be in shortly to check on you. I'll be right back."

She made some notes in my chart, smiled again and walked out of the room. I took the few moments I had to myself to get my thoughts together. I finally did it. I thought again. I already felt like a new woman. I was so excited.

"Hey, sleepyhead."

It was Tiff coming in with a huge slice of pizza on a paper plate in one hand and a drink in the other.

"I'm ready to go home," I told her as she sat in the chair next to my bed.

"I just saw the doctor in the hallway and he said he'll be releasing you soon."

"That's good," I said while eyeing her pizza.

"Pepperoni and cheese," she said as she took a bite.

"I haven't eaten a thing since last night. When do I get to eat?"

"As soon as you get home. Things like Jell-o, broth, ice cream and juice. Nothing heavy for awhile," Dr Horowitz said walking in and checking out my chart.

"No pizza, uh?" I joked.

"Not just yet." He gave me a warm smile and patted my arm. "How do you feel?"

"I feel alright. I have a little discomfort. It's not as bad as I thought."

"Nothing is as bad as we think. The discomfort is normal."

Just then the nurse returned with some pain pills while Dr. Horowitz checked me out. He gave me my instructions on the after care and my prescription. After getting me home in bed, Tiff fixed me some chicken noodle soup, crackers and gave me a glass of 7-Up and got me my mail. I searched through the stack of mail until I found what I was looking for, a card from Perry. Perry has really been a breath of fresh air for me and now that I've had my surgery, I'm hoping things will only get better for us.

"Baby, I'm glad your surgery went well."

"I am too. Tiff has been a great help and I've enjoyed her staying with me these last couple of nights."

"Did she tell you about Rico?"

"Yes. The classes he took while he's been locked up knocked a lot of time off of his sentences."

"I saw him yesterday and he said after all of his paper work goes through he'll be home."

"That's truly a blessing."

"Maybe something like that will happen to me. You never know around here. They treat you any way they want. You can all of a sudden have time added to your sentence or have time taken away. It all depends on how they feel."

"You get treated like cattle. If you were to come home, I'd fix you a good home cooked meal, have you a nice hot bath ready and pamper you like a baby."

"Don't tell me that, you make me want to break out and run straight to you." He laughed. The automated operator came on telling us our time was almost up.

"I love you," he said.

"I love you too," I replied.

We both reminded each other to check the mail and we'd talk again on Sunday.

Saturday afternoon Lynn came to visit with a ton of food for lunch. She brought fried chicken, biscuits, apple butter, macaroni and cheese salad, string beans, corn-on-the-cob, cheese cubes, grapes, strawberries and for dessert a New York style cheesecake.

"Plenty of food means plenty of gossip," I said taking the food out of the bags.

"You know that's right," she said reaching for plates and glasses.

We piled some of everything on our plates and went into the living room. By the end of the meal, not only was I full but I had a napkin wiping away tears from laughing so hard.

"Things are still crazy." I said catching my breath.

"Honey, I hope you didn't expect anything to change."

"Our viewers think it's a soap opera on screen, if only they knew what happens behind the camera."

"Time sure flies when you're having fun," Lynn said looking at her watch. "It's almost 1:30 and I promised my sister I'd help her pick out wallpaper for the baby's room."

She began gathering her dishes and used napkins from the coffee table.

"Leave all of that there," I said getting up from the couch. "You've done enough by bringing me lunch and keeping me company. I'm bored stiff not doing anything around here, let me have some kind of fun today."

"All right." Lynn said and grabbed her purse. "Don't strain yourself. If you need me, call."

"Yes, mother," I joked and hugged her.

"I'll call you tomorrow to check on you." She said putting her jacket on.

"Trust me, I'll be here."

I watched as she got into her car and drove off. I decided to take a nap first and get to the kitchen later. When Lynn called the next day she had me on speaker phone located in a conference room at the studio. I was happy to talk to everyone and they all wished me a speedy recovery. Later, Tiff called to check on me.

"What's up?" She asked.

"Nothing much. Lynn called and had everybody on

the speaker phone at the studio. That's the most excitement I've had all day."

"That's all the excitement you need. Look, I was calling to tell you I'll be over late. I'm going to go home first and do some stuff around the house to get ready for Rico's homecoming party."

"Girl, you can stay at home. I'll be fine."

"I don't want to leave you alone," she whined.

"Florence Nightingale you've been over here all week. You have plenty to do with Rico coming home. I'll be fine. If anything serious happens, which I doubt, I'll call you."

"I'm concerned that's all."

"I know and I appreciate that. There's been no swelling, no bleeding and if I have any pain I have this giant bottle of nasty pain pills."

"I'll check on you once I get settled. I'm going to go grab me something to eat before my lunch is over."

"Talk to you later."

Thank goodness for my girl. She's always there for me and I'm glad she was here for this major event in my life. It's good to have someone in your corner. I hope Perry will be that someone after I tell him.

There were purple and gold streamers and balloons everywhere. Those are Rico's favorite colors, purple for loyalty and gold for prosperity. The house was packed, the music was jamming, the drinks were flowing and there was plenty of food. The menu consisted of fried chicken wings, grilled steaks, hamburgers, hot dogs, greens, baked macaroni and cheese, potato salad, rolls, string beans, deviled eggs, baked beans, fruit, veggie and cheese platters, a lemon cake, a chocolate cake and three sweet potato pies for dessert. It was a wonderful Spring afternoon. The sun was warm and bright and the air was fresh. All of the guests were dressed to the nines. Everyone was enjoying themselves.

"What's up sexy?" Rico's slow, smooth voice asked me.

"You," I replied giving him a tight hug. "You're looking good."

"It's that prison workout, baby. You gotta try and keep your mind off of where you at and working out helps. Know what I'm saying?" He filled his cup with some fruit punch.

"I can imagine."

Rico was more muscular than before. His chest stuck out, his arms were bigger, his neck was thick, but he still had that sweet, warm smile.

"You been helping my girl hold down the fort?" he said as he continued to pile wings onto a paper plate.

"For sure. You know that's my girl too."

"I heard that. Oh yeah, Perry sends his love. You're all he talks about. I was like damn man, chill out." He gave a little laugh.

"Perry is sweet. I really enjoy talking and writing to him. I can't wait until it's his turn to come home." I put a fresh trash bag in the trash can.

"Give it time, he'll be out before you know it."

Tiff came through the kitchen door.

"Baby, everybody's looking for you. I should have known you'd be in here. That's your third plate." She wrapped her arms around his waist.

"You know I ain't had no real food in a minute, Boo. Everybody's gotta wait." He kissed her forehead.

"The dog is off the porch!"

Rico's so called friend G-Money came busting through into the kitchen. Following him were two more of Rico's other buddies, Tyrone and Kane.

"What's happenin', fellas?" Rico shouted giving all of them ghetto hugs and high fives.

"Look at this muthafucka," Tyrone said, "you big as hell."

86

I noticed Tiff rolling her eyes at G-Money and his crew. G-Money was a drug dealer deep into the game and she had already told me he was the last person she wanted Rico around. She was going to try to keep Rico out of that lifestyle once and for all. The fellas finally realized Tiff and I were in the kitchen too.

"What's up ladies?" Kane said with his gold tooth waving from between his big lips.

"Hey," I said and continued to clean the kitchen. Tiff spoke up loud and bold.

"Grab yourselves something to eat and get out of the kitchen. It's too tight up in here as it is."

"Damn, Tiffany, you ain't got to be all mean," Tyrone said.

"Well you can get the hell out if you don't like it!" Tiff replied.

"That's enough," Rico cut in. "Ya'll go ahead and get your plates and let's chill on the patio."

Once everyone was out, it was just Tiff and me.

"I can't stand them," she said angrily. "Rico bet not think about hanging with those bitches or we're through." She threw a dish towel in the sink.

"Let him hang with them for now and talk to him about it later. Enjoy the fact that your man is home and that's what everybody is here to celebrate. Don't let those fools ruin a good moment." I touched her arm to try and calm her down.

"You're right, Koffie. I worked hard to get everything and everybody together. I'm going to enjoy myself but make sure he doesn't leave with those bastards. Thanks for keeping me on track,." she said in a calmer voice.

"That's what friends are for," I said hugging her. "Now let's go see which one of the relatives has gotten the drunkest so far."

We both laughed and headed out to be with the rest of the guests.

"Man. Baby, it sounds like you guys had a good time and good food."

"I wish you could have been there."

"I'll be home soon," Perry was assuring me.

"I can't wait. We're going to have our own private party."

"That's what I like to hear," he laughed. "Enough about me, how have you been feeling?"

"I've been doing well. I had a follow up appointment with my doctor last week and I've healed up great. I'm still going to stay off from work for the next few weeks. It's no need of me rushing back, plus I can get some things done here around the house I've wanted to do for awhile."

"I understand. I'm glad everything worked out even though you won't tell me why you needed the surgery."

"You'll find out when you're supposed to," I told him.

"I guess I'll have to wait then," he said.

I thought about how much I hated keeping secrets, but he really was going to have to wait until the time was right.

The Monday before I was due back at work, Tiff and I had made all day appointments that Saturday at Blue's Groove to get done up from the feet up. We had already had our facials and our hair done and we were getting our manicures and pedicures.

"Foxy Blue hooked us up again," Tiff stated.

"It was way past time for it. I can't believe I've been walking around looking raggedy about the head."

I looked at my image in the mirror on the wall and I was looking too hot now. Tiffany was looking back to her normal self as well. Ever since Rico's return she's been much happier. She has a vibrant, healthy glow that wasn't there when he was locked up.

"Tiff, you look good girl," I commented.

"I feel good too. Rico is like a new man. We talk so much more now than we did before. We talk about everything. He's opened up a lot to me. He lets me know where he's going and if he's been gone too long, he'll call me. He's even talked about us joining church."

"What? Rico has changed. That sounds good. How are things going with G-Money and his boys?" I asked.

"He's only talked to them maybe twice since the party. He's been going to these classes his probation officer signed him up for. Next week he has an interview with a construction company. He said he doesn't have time for G-Money. You know I'm happy to hear that."

"Who can blame him? I forgot he used to work in construction back in the day before he got caught up in dealing."

"I hope he gets this job. Keep your fingers crossed," she instructed.

"Rico is a good man and he loves you."

"Thank you for keeping me sane during his time away."

"I'd do it all over again if I had to. But I don't think we'll be going through this anymore."

"I know that's right. Next time you talk to Perry, Rico said have him call the house. How has Perry been anyway?"

"He's doing good. He's hoping to be out soon too. We've already agreed since he really doesn't have any place to go, he can move in with me whenever he gets out."

I looked out the corner out of my eye to catch Tiff's reaction.

"What?" she screamed. "I knew it would work. Congratulations!"

"Ladies, we're going to give you a few minutes to let your nails dry and you'll be free to go," the nail technician informed us.

"Thank you," we both responded. Tiff and I continued to talk and had plans to go to lunch after leaving Blue's Groove. We were also going shopping and it was a beautiful Spring day to do so. I felt like something good was going to happen.

My first week back to Every Life was hectic, but I was happy to be in the swing of things. The cast was extremely happy to have me back. Obviously my replacement was hard to get along with. Lynn was the first to let me know.

"I told you she was a bitch before you went on your leave. My God, she thought she knew everything and she knew absolutely nothing. Whatever cheap foundation she used broke me out. I've never had that happen before. I wouldn't be surprised if she put something in it to make me break out. It was no secret that I didn't like her, I was so tempted to call you."

"Snap out of it!" I said putting both of my hands on her shoulders. "I'm back now."

"You have to promise to never leave again," she gave me a warm hug.

"I promise," I said playfully throwing my right hand in the air.

"Welcome back," she replied and hopped into my make-up chair.

Sunday morning I had just finished cooking breakfast and was pouring my milk when the phone rang. I picked it up anxiously. After accepting the collect call, our date was on. Perry sounded excited.

"Baby, I've got great news."

"Calm down and tell me what happened."

He took a deep breath and began speaking a little slower.

"First, I graduate this Friday with my degree."

"Congratulations, college man!" I screamed.

"Which is good because I'm coming home!" he shouted.

"What?" I dropped my toast. "When? How?" I yelled with excitement.

"I got a visit from my attorney. The evidence they used in my trial was not mine. My evidence had been lost so they really have nothing on me." He gave a hearty laugh. "I'll be home soon!"

"Perry, that's wonderful. We finally get to put our plan into action. I can't wait to tell Tiffany and Rico."

We stayed on the phone until our time expired and he promised to call me if there was any more news. After we hung up, my mind immediately began to race. What if he was just talking to me while he was locked up? He may get out and not want to be with me. A man fresh out of prison isn't going to want to be on "lockdown" again when he's released. Anybody can change, right? Look at Rico, he's talking about going to church. In the past, going to church to Rico meant picking up a three piece dinner from Church's Chicken.

"Enough!" I said aloud. "Take it one step at a time. The man hasn't even made it out of the prison gate yet."

I took a couple of deep breaths and began to plan our first face-to-face meeting.

Two weeks later I was picking Perry up from the Greyhound Bus Station downtown. When he walked into the bus station I automatically knew it was him. The photos he had sent did him no justice. He had on a nice pair of loose fitting jeans, a button up one pocket shirt that was tucked and had the first two buttons undone, exposing a white tee shirt. He carried a blue duffel bag. He apparently knew it was me too. He took a quick look around and once he spotted me, walked over in my direction.

"Well hello, Ms. Hamilton," he said in that deep, sexy voice I had become familiar with over time. "It's finally nice to meet you."

He gave a gorgeous smile and I noticed a dimple on his left cheek.

"Mr. St. James, it's a pleasure meeting you too," I said in a low sultry voice.

He stepped forward and gave me a sweet kiss on the lips. That one kiss was full of electricity and I wanted to melt right there. I then heard a garbled male voice over the public address system announcing a bus leaving from gate ten going to Atlanta. That's what brought me back to reality. I gave a little laugh and so did Perry as we both looked around the crowded station.

"Let's get out of here," I said.

"I'm right behind you," he said following me through the crowd and to my car.

I told him to throw his bag into the backseat and informed him we were headed to Tiff and Rico's place for a cookout we planned for him. Watching him during the car ride was like watching a little kid in a candy store. It was a beautiful, warm, sunny day and we had the windows down and the radio blaring. I figured I'd have all night to talk to him, I wanted to enjoy the moment. When we pulled up on Tiff's street, I turned the radio down and told him Tiff and Rico lived at the end of the block.

"That was the best ride of my life," Perry said smiling hard. "It's a beautiful day to be out, breathing in fresh air, listening to some jams and being in the company of a lovely woman." He squeezed my hand.

We pulled into the driveway and parked. I noticed him pulling his shirt off and throwing it in the backseat with his bag. I wanted to fall out. Those strong, broad shoulders fitting into that tee shirt like he was poured into it. He had a small waist and a nice flat stomach. Exactly what I like. I turned to walk towards the door and gave myself a smile thinking about what I had. I prayed

I'd be able to keep him. I knocked on the door and Tiff answered with all smiles. We hugged as usual and I could smell the aroma of the food grilling on the patio. Tiffany, this is Perry. Perry, this is Rico's girlfriend, Tiffany. I introduced. I stepped aside and let them meet.

"I feel like I already know you," Perry said giving her a hug.

"I feel the same too," she replied.

"Damn man, you ain't been out twenty-four hours and you already trying to steal my woman," Rico said coming in from the patio carrying a long fork and laughing.

"What's up, man?" Perry said laughing back.

"What's up with you, dawg?" Rico asked hugging Perry.

"I'm trying to make sure I'm not dreaming man. I can't believe I'm out."

"I know that feeling," Rico replied. "Come on out back ya'll."

We sat out on the patio eating, drinking and talking until it got dark. After coming in, Tiff and I went into the kitchen to clean up while Perry and Rico sat in the living room with some music on and talking. By the time Perry and I left it was after 11:00 that night.

"Well, come in," I said letting him into the front hall. "You can leave your bag there for now and I'll show you around the house."

I started with the kitchen, then the bathroom, moved on to my room and the living room. Since the living room was connected to the dining room, I made that last. I had bought a bouquet of assorted flowers and around the table on the floor were different colored balloons. On the table next to the flowers was a cake that had "Welcome Home" on it.

"This is where I sat and ate breakfast with you on Sundays."

"Baby, this is beautiful. You didn't have to do this."

"I know. I wanted to do this for you."

Before I could say anything else he took me in his strong arms and gave me a long passionate kiss. I could feel him growing against me. When the kiss ended, he said in that hypnotic voice, "I've been waiting for a long time to do that." I couldn't even respond. My mind was running wild with thoughts of the things I wanted to happen. We stared into each other's eyes and he took my hand and lead me to the bedroom where he laid me down. He removed my high heels and slowly but firmly massaged my feet. I was so happy I had gotten a pedicure. He knelt down at the end of the bed and kissed each toe. All ten was blessed with a kiss from his sweet lips. He massaged my calves and moved up to my thighs. I laid still and closed my eyes. When he got to the top of my blue jean shorts, he unbuttoned and unzipped them and planted a cool kiss on my stomach. He continued pushing my shirt up until it was over my head and lucky for us I had worn a front hook bra. He took two fingers and released my waiting breasts and began to suck on each nipple. I became alive and took his shirt off, rubbing my hands along his masculine back and shoulders, around his neck and through his hair. He kneeled back in the bed and removed my shorts and panties.

"Beautiful," he said softly.

He removed his jeans and underwear and there it was, his long manhood, hard and waiting to be taken in. I couldn't wait any longer and neither could Perry. Neither one of us had made love in so long to anyone I was surprised we went as slow and sensual as we did. The real show was about to begin though. He entered the secret garden, gave a little moan and slowly pushed forward. I moaned and grabbed onto him and pushed my body towards him. The rhythm started and it felt good. I cried out and we clutched onto one another. My goodness I was going to explode. My body was on fire. I

94

grabbed around his neck and hung on for the ride. When he thrust deeper the sensation of the moment over took both of us. After a few strokes we both came with great force. I didn't know what to say. This had gone further much faster than I expected. I let this situation get out of hand and I felt sick.

"Baby, that was good," he said planting a kiss on my neck. "I'm going to the bathroom, okay?" His words brought me back to life.

"Sure, if you need a towel or a washcloth look in the linen closet in the hall."

He leaned down and gave me another kiss.

"Thanks, beautiful."

When I heard him close the bathroom door I immediately got up, put on my robe and went into my closet. I had to tell him. I can't live a lie. The tears began to blur my vision as I searched through the back of my closet. I knew what I needed and I pushed past my clothes, shoes and boots. Some of the clothes slipped off of the hangers into a cluttered pile on the floor. I continued to cry and tried to feel on top of my shelf. I shoved aside scarves, hats, purses and articles of clothing. I touched what I was looking for and pulled the medium sized safe box down to me. I held onto it by the handle and felt the bottom to make sure the key was still taped to the bottom. It was. I climbed over all of the piles of clothes I had made looking for this safe box. I came out of the closet back into the bedroom where the air was cooler and sat on the bed with tears still coming down my face. I took the key and unlocked the box. I cried even harder, I hadn't opened this box in years, but this was something that needed to be done. If I was going to live the life I wanted to live, I had to be honest with the person I had fallen in love with. Perry walked in.

"Baby, I hope you don't mind, I decided to take a shower..." He froze. "Baby, why are you crying?" I couldn't say anything. I sat there trembling.

"Did I do something wrong? Baby, do you want me to leave?" He sounded just as scared as I was. I shook my head no.

"I need to tell you something." I sobbed. I started pulling the contents of the safe box out and laying them in front of Perry on the bed. The first photo was of a baby dressed in a blue sailor outfit. The next was a little boy in a cowboy outfit blowing out candles on a birthday cake. Another was a photo of a little boy in a baseball uniform holding a bat. Various pictures of this same boy in various photos as he got older.

"You have a son? You didn't have to hide him from me. That's no big deal. Where is he?" Perry said calmly.

"No, no, no! That's me!" I blurted out tears pouring down my face still. I slid my original birth certificate towards him.

"Thomas Eugene," he read aloud. "I don't understand. What are you talking about?"

I begin to explain.

"Growing up I've always felt different. I never felt I belonged with the other little boys. I guess somehow they knew I was different too. I was never allowed to play with them and every kid in the neighborhood always teased me. I dealt with that for a long time." He continued to listen calmly. "The older I got the more feminine I became. My own family rejected me. To make a long story short, I decided after I graduated from high school, I would leave that small, close-minded town and live my life as what I was suppose to be, as a woman. Tiffany has always known. She's been my support system since we were children. No one else knows what I've been through but Tiff. Rico doesn't even know." I tried to compose myself. "The operation was my final step. I am now complete. Everything is in place. This is now who I am."

I had told him everything. What more could I say? We both sat in silence for awhile then he finally spoke.

"I really don't know what to say. I'm in shock."

He flipped through the photos of the me I used to be again.

"What can I do?" He put the photos back into the safe box. "I don't know this Thomas Eugene person. I met Koffie Hamilton and that's who I fell in love with. Thomas is your past like my past is at the correctional facility." He stood up and re-wrapped the towel around his waist. "Listen, all I want is a good woman to love me and one I can love back. I need a woman to build a future with and so far from what I know and see, you're that woman and hopefully I'm that man for you." He pulled me into his comforting arms. I cried again he just held me.

"Thank you for not being angry at me and leaving."

"No, thank you for being you and for being honest with me. Let's put this away and leave the past in the past for both of us. Let's start working on our future."

I put the box away and thought maybe at a later time I'd destroy all of the contents once and for all. Then again, maybe I'd keep everything as a reminder of who I once was and how I became the person I am today. Perry broke my concentration.

"Go clean your face and let's go get some of that cake at our special place. Then maybe we can come back and recreate what we just did," he smiled at me.

"I'm right with you." I smiled back.

The next day Tiff and I met for lunch and I told her everything that happened.

"Koffie, that is wonderful. I'm too happy for you and Perry."

"I told him until he found a job, I would continue to perform at the Golden Shower for the extra money."

"Is he going to see you perform? I mean, he does know it's a gay bar doesn't he?"

"He knows. I'm going to perform last so he can come in late and not have to stay long. I don't want him to feel uncomfortable. He's been so understanding, you know what I mean? I've given him enough to swallow, I don't want him to choke."

Tiff laughed.

"Well, I have good news too. Rico and I joined church last Sunday and I think he's going to propose soon. He's been talking about marriage a lot lately," she grinned.

"Girl, that is great!" I shouted. "Things have really worked out."

After lunch I went back to work feeling better than ever. I had so much to look forward to, a new man who loves and understands me, a new life, a whole new me and my best friend getting married. If Rico is talking about it, he's going to do it. Life is good if we just let it flow.

What I Want

I just want to
Kiss you
Hug you
Smell you
Love you
Hold you
Squeeze you
Taste you
Give you what you want when you need it
Remind you when you haven't had it

I just want to
Eat you
Drink you
Lick you off my soul
Show you how and why as I lick between your thighs
Slave you
Sweat you
Hurt you with pleasure
Fuck you and love you at the same time
Then sit back and remember,
With you,
I just want to

Take Advantage

Wrap yourself around me, your fantasy come to life
I'm all yours
Your private whore
Letting go of every vice

Lighting the internal flames
As the heat begins to rise
Passion building, excitement boiling
In front of your very eyes

Naked thoughts waking up and stretching comfortably
wide
Releasing that sexual beast
Can't wait until you're inside
No longer in a suit and tie
but tied with scarves of lace
As much as we'd like to rush this moment
We're keeping a steady pace
Keeping secrets
Unlocking secrets
Victoria's secret
I'm the secret
Sweet, ripe and juicy is how my treasure taste
Keeping up, getting your fill, allowing nothing to go to
waste
Touching,
Teasing,
Sexually pleasing,
Wicked conversations put your mind into a zone
Engaging in real life fantasy, makes you tremble and
brings a moan
Hot,
Sweaty,
Funky sex

An erotic workout taken step by step
On the rise and staying high,
Taking advantage of this moment
Not letting it slip by..

Stripped Raw

"This is my best friend," Darrius said as he introduced me to some of his co-workers. "She's just like one of my sisters." He told his jealous girlfriend. "She and I aren't like that." He informed his loud talking, joke-cracking uncles.

Darrius is right. When it comes to our relationship I am the best friend, just like a sister and it never has been "like that" with us. Let's see Darrius and I have known each other since our first year in college. We actually met at the Chicken Shack, an off campus restaurant where students went to eat after the school cafeteria was closed. My roommate Brenda was dating Darnell who happened to be Darrius' roommate. I had already been peeping Darrius out in Freshmen Orientation, English 101 and Algebra way before Brenda introduced us. He was fine then and as we've grown into adulthood, he's become even better looking. He's a pecan sandy complexion with short black wavy hair. He stands six feet two inches and weighs two hundred solid pounds. He has a very toned body and you can't help but melt when he stares at you with those dark, deep-set brown eyes. Have I mentioned how intelligent he is? Darrius is very business minded. He's started his own food supply distribution company and has been very successful throughout the state. I'm so proud of him, yet so angry with him all at once. You have to understand I've been with him through thick and thin. Through the break ups and the make-ups. Through business ventures that have failed to the ones that have survived. I've been there when he was broke to when he was on the top of his game. I'm there through all of the tornadoes and the rainbows. I'm always there, as his friend. We've been to breakfast, lunch, dinner and all of the meals in between, as friends. He's spent many nights at my place and me at his, as friends.

We've been out to clubs, house parties and get-togethers, as friends. We've spent holidays with one another's families, as friends.

And here it is, ten years after college graduation and we're still just friends. I can't put all of the blame on Darrius. I guess I have given him a reason to not look at me like I would like for him to. I know Darrius has never been attracted to what I call a fluffy woman. Or, what the rest of the world calls fat. Okay, being 5"7' and 200 pounds does not put you in a size five dress. I know I'm cute, hell, that's the only compliment a fat girl gets. "You have such a pretty face." Both strangers and everyone I know has said before. Thanks, if that isn't a slap in the pretty face I have I don't know what is. It's like saying, "Your face is pleasant, but the rest of you, DAMN!" Let me not mention the dumb question people always ask. "Why don't you just lose the weight?" Sometimes I wish I could respond with, "Oh, I don't know, I kinda like the pregnant look even though I'm not." Don't people know if losing weight was really that easy I would have lost the weight a long time ago? I have tried Slim-Fast, (better known as slim slow) Weight Watchers, Jenny Craig and plenty of other pills, drinks and fads. I know I've looked for the quick way to lose weight and not necessarily the most nutritional or the healthiest way. I know losing weight would be better for my overall health. It would lower my blood pressure, lessen my chances of heart disease and diabetes but most importantly, make me look sexy. Not that I'm not sexy now, I just want to be sexy in a smaller package. That's why I've made this pledge, this promise to do it! To stick with a plan and lose weight!

This became my mission the last official weekend of the Summer. Every year Darrius, Darnell, Brenda and I throw this jamming end of the summer bar-b-que with old college friends, family and whoever else decides to come by for the event. Every year it gets better and bigger. It has gotten to the point where we hire a disc jockey and have the event catered. And every year Darrius invites a new somebody he claims he's involved with more serious then the last one. This year it was Carmen. Short, light and damn near white, long hair, wearing high heels and something short and tight. She must be the twin of the last girl he was seeing who must have been the twin of the one before that. And so on, and so on and so on. Damn, where does he find these girls? I can't do a thing but shake my head. Of course I always get to meet them. I'm the sister, the best friend remember?

"Yanni, I want you to meet Carmen, Danielle, Rachael, Misty, Asia, India, Gabrielle." The list goes on and on. The other thing they all have in common outside of their looks is that they never last.

"She was beautiful, Yanni, she just couldn't hold my interest." He would say after he dumped another one. "If she were as smart as she was fine, she would have been the perfect woman." He'd comment.

"Yanni, I can tell you that girl could do all type of tricks in bed. Too bad she couldn't trick me into thinking she was smart." He'd tell me. I would ask him the same question after each break up, "Why do you keep picking them cute and dumb?" I'd laugh.

"Just the kind of luck I'm cursed with," he'd joke.

As you can see, Darrius needs an intelligent and fine woman. That's where me and my plan come in. I've got the intelligent part down pat. I was valedictorian of our graduating class. It's the other part I need to work on. Plus, what other woman knows Darrius better than me? There is none. Once I made the decision to put this plan in action, I had to make myself scarce with Brenda, Darnell and especially Darrius.

When friends and family began to question my whereabouts, I told everyone I started tutoring and volunteering at the Education Center with the youth again. Everyone knows how hectic my schedule could be during the school year. This gave me time to work with a nutritionist and yes, even a personal trainer. My nutritionist Sherri is cool. She has taught me how to cut out the "bad" sweet stuff, which I needed to do whether thick or thin. I now snack on animal crackers, instead of potato chips and for dessert, I have fresh fruit and angel food cake instead of a chunk of chocolate cake and ice cream. I eat fresh vegetables instead of canned, lean meat and low fat everything. With Sherri being my food guide, the transition has been easier than expected. Plus, she has me keeping a food diary and I can't bring myself to cheat. Now my personal trainer, Greg, sometimes I wish I could cheat him out of taking a few breaths. I have to admit, although there are days when I've wanted to take a barbell to the back of his head, he has proven to be a huge part of my transformation. I can hear him now in that California surfer dude voice.

"Take a few minutes to stretch and warm up. Drink plenty of water during and after your workouts. Proper form means a proper workout."

Each and every tip Greg gave, I took. Some nights I don't think I'm going to make it to my car after a workout with him. My legs are so weak and my muscles are so sore I just want to crawl out to the parking lot and pass out in the backseat of my car. Instead, I keep giving myself pep talks. *I've made it this far, only a few more steps to go. No pain, no gain.* Then during those times when I really feel drained, I go into Nike mode and tell myself, *Just do it!*

With the holidays fast approaching, I have to figure out a game plan to continue avoiding Darrius and the crew.

"Girl, I haven't seen you in a thousand Sundays, I know you're coming over for Thanksgiving." His silky, smooth voice penetrated through the phone to touch my soul during one of our many phone calls.

"We're all packing up and driving to Aunt Geri's for Thanksgiving." I lied trying to sound normal, not letting the images in my head come out in my voice.

"Ya'll are driving from St. Louis all the way to Atlanta?" he asked in a high pitched voice.

"Mom said she wants to do something different this year. She said it's time somebody else cooks instead of her. So we'll be renting two vans and heading south."

"I wish I could go. Atlanta is the spot. I know you're going to get your party on while you're there."

"You know I'll have to do just that," I replied. Thank goodness I was able to lie my way out of Thanksgiving, Christmas, and New Year's Eve. Damn, I even lied my way out of a Valentine's singles party. This was becoming habit forming. Darrius did keep me posted on the happenings with everything and everybody because we talked on the phone and e-mailed each other almost daily. I kept telling myself, just a little while longer.

Here it is six months later and everyday when I look in the mirror I have to re-introduce myself to myself because I still can't believe the image that's looking back at me is me. Last night before my workout Greg said he needed to weigh me to update my chart.

"Whoa dude! A total loss of forty-five pounds! Awesome!" he shouted sounding totally valley for sure.

I couldn't believe it. I was so shocked I began crying. After consoling me and reminding me of how hard I've worked and how much I deserved this, Greg fell into his West Coast drill sergeant routine. As strange as it sounds, I was beginning to like this routine he and I had. After my workout I decided to reward myself for doing such a good job with my weight loss program. I stopped off at Baskin-Robbins ice cream shop and purchased one scoop of raspberry cheese Louise. It's a low fat cheesecake yogurt with raspberry cheesecake pieces and graham cracker bits swirled with a raspberry ribbon. I was a good girl and got it in a cup, not on a cone. I've learned how to reward myself and at the same time not deprive myself of the foods I love.

"Moderation is the key." Sherri always tells me.

While driving home in my state of euphoria, I noticed bright neon lights with a pair of flashing pink panties and a scrolling marquee. The marquee rolled the words "Pink Panties Gentlemen's Club" continuously. I almost choked on my ice cream. This is the club Darrius, Darnell and their friends have been known to come to on occasions. According to the fellas, Pink Panties has the best strippers in town.

"Clean with no stretch marks and no bullet wounds," I can hear Darnell saying.

I've been on this street many times and I've never noticed Pink Panties. I pulled into the gas station that was on the next corner across from the strip club. I stood outside my car eating my ice cream as I filled my gas tank. I couldn't keep my eyes off of the building. I was trying to see each person as they walked in the club. I wondered what type of men they were. Were they perverts constantly having nasty sex thoughts? Or, were they rich businessmen married to old frumpy, conservative wives? What about horny college boys trying to get a foot into manhood? Either way, whenever the door swung open I'd strain my eyes trying to see past the oversized burly bouncer at the door. I couldn't see a thing. The click from the gas handle alerted me my tank was full and brought me back to life. Next thing I knew I was standing in front of the bouncer asking how much it cost to get into the club.

"Ladies get in free every night," he answered in a gruffly voice, while holding the door open for me to walk in.

"Thanks," I said walking into the main doorway. I stood at the door for a few minutes just taking in the view. It was not what I had expected at all. The club was dimly lit and to my left was a long bar that stretched from the front to the back of the club. Tall, black stools with high backs were lined in front of it. There were three bartenders taking orders and making drinks. To my right were several round and square tables with two and four chairs at each one. Each table was covered with a white cloth and had a burning candle in a circular candleholder. Directly in front of me was the stage. Men were scattered throughout the club. Dancing for the men that sat around the stage was a petite white woman with blonde hair that hung to her waist. She was wearing shoes that were at least five inches tall with a clear top and silver spiked heels. She had on a silver belly chain that connected to her belly ring, red G-string panties and had huge breasts that stood at attention more than any soldier in the U.S. military. All those tits and no ass, typical white girl build. I knew those breasts could not have been real, and by the looks of it, the way men were tucking and throwing money on stage for her, I could see how she paid for them.

"Would you like anything to drink?" a female voice asked me.

I realized I was still standing in the doorway. I turned to a smiling topless waitress, with long red hair. She was wearing black motorcycle boots, a pair of leather chaps and black thongs, holding a round drink tray.

"Um...yeah. I guess I'll have a rum and coke," I responded nervously. I couldn't think of anything else to order and I needed some type of drink that was going to keep my nerves calm so I could get through this. "I'll be sitting over there," I told her pointing to an empty square table near the corner in the back of the room.

"All right," she said cheerfully. "I'll be back in a minute with your drink." She smiled and headed towards the bar.

I made my way through the few men that was sitting in that area and tried to get comfortable until the waitress came back with my drink. Even though it was still pretty early for a Friday night, the club had a good crowd. The disc jockey was jamming too. The waitress returned with my drink and a napkin so I took a sip and got settled in to observe the show. I watched how each dancer got on stage and how she worked the men, not only with her skills at dancing, but she also had to have a fun and bubbly personality. She had to make each customer feel like he was the only one in the club. The dancers worked hard for their money. I noticed every once in awhile a dancer would lead a man by his hand behind a pair of red curtains on the other side of the club. It must have been where they gave their private lap dances. This club really is nice. I can see why Darrius and the guys liked coming here. It was clean, everyone seemed to be relaxed, the d.j. was jamming, the girls were very entertaining and the bartender hooked it up with my drink. The next dancer that came onto the stage was introduced as Heavenly. Now I'm quite sure that could not have been the name her momma gave her. When the music started, she came from backstage with a mission. She was a sista through and through. She had a body that made me say "Damn!" She had a dark, smooth complexion, long black hair that hung to the middle of her back and almond shaped eyes. Her soft facial features complimented her full lips. Not to mention the ghetto booty sistas are known to have. That girl worked that stage like it wasn't nothing. Every eye in the club was on her. Men flocked to the stage like ants to candy on a hot sidewalk during the Summer time. She made her way around each side of the stage dropping it like it was hot and picking it up like it was cold. She wore white six-inch boots that laced up to the knees, a sky blue thong and a thin sheer white robe that was about ankle length. When her second song was played, she removed the robe and worked the brass pole in the center of the stage. She mesmerized everyone with how she made her booty bounce. First, the left cheek, then the right, then both at the same time. She laughed when she rubbed a man's face into her breasts. She really amazed us all when she had another man lay on his back with a dollar bill in his mouth and she stood over him and removed it from his mouth without using her hands. She then took a leap onto the pole like a cat to a tree, swung around twice and twirled until she was upside down and sliding slowly to the floor like she was being poured out of the ceiling. By the end of the act, I knew she was the one.

This idea came to me as I was pumping gas. With all of this weight I've lost and my confidence level growing, what would be the perfect way to show the new me off to Darrius? Perform a strip routine! I figured if I found the right dancer to teach me some moves, I would definitely get the attention of Darrius. I now have to ask Heavenly if this is something she would be willing to do. That is if she will take me under her wing as her student. After watching her make her rounds through the club to some of the customers and taking a few back for private dances, I thought I'd catch her when she came out from her last private dance. I approached her nervously.

"Excuse me, Heavenly." I said over the music. "My name is Yanni and I was wondering if I could speak to you for a minute."

"Does this have something to do with a man?" she asked looking me up and down.

"Yes. I mean no." I couldn't answer her correctly.

"Sweetheart, I don't date or sleep with any of these men from the club, so if you think me and your man..."

"No, no, that's not it," I said cutting her off. "It's nothing like that. Look, do you mind if we go back over to my table? I really need your help." I was still nervous.

"I guess. I'll give you a few minutes. Where are you sitting?"

I pointed out the table and lead the way. When we got to the table I began to speak.

"My name is Yanni," I said reintroducing myself. "I'm not quite sure how to say this, so I'm just going to come right out and say it." I then explained to her how I recently lost forty-five pounds and the man I lost the weight for hasn't seen me since the new me developed. I informed her I wanted to surprise him by performing a strip tease. I told her I just needed somebody to teach me how to strip. "And that's where you come in. I'm willing to pay you $2500 if you become my teacher."

She stared at me for a moment with a blank look on her face. The music was still blaring through the speakers. More customers had come in and a girl named Natasha was now on stage. Heavenly finally spoke.

"Damn! You want to pay me $2500 to teach you to dance?"

"Well, not dance, but strip," I corrected her.

"I've had plenty offers, but none ever like this."

"Well, will you do it?" I asked. I was anxious to know her answer.

"When would you want to start?" she asked.

"As soon as possible," I replied.

"The club is closed on Mondays for deliveries and inventory. I would be able to use the club then. If you're serious, be here with half of my money around 5pm," as she pointed a long red fingernail at me.

I let out a long sigh of relief. I couldn't believe it, I was

111

going to learn how to strip.

"I guess we have a deal." I stuck my hand out for her to shake it.

"No, we have a deal when I see you here on Monday with half of my money," she said standing up and leaving my hand hanging in mid air.

"Alright, I guess I'll see you Monday then. What should I bring?" I asked standing up too.

"Something comfortable to dance in and heels. Tall heels."

With that said, she headed to the bar and started talking and laughing with a couple of white men that looked like they just left the office. I then left the club and headed home to search through my closet to see what type of high heels I had that would be good to dance in.

When Monday came around, at the end of my workday, I ran out of the office so fast I left a trail of smoke behind me. Over the weekend I had gone to one of those adult stores where they sell porn movies, sex toys, clothes and other things and purchased a pair of black six-inch stilettos with the toes and heels out and a strap around the ankles. I pulled into the back parking lot of the Pink Panties club around 5:20. I grabbed my duffel bag off of the passenger seat and quickly ran in. I was trying to hurry because one, I was running late and two, I didn't want anyone I knew to be driving by seeing me going into a strip club. I would never be able to explain that. When I stepped into Pink Panties it was no real difference from my visit Friday. The lighting was still low and the music was cranked. There were a few people gathered at the bar.

"Here she is!" I heard Heavenly shout out. "For a minute I thought you weren't coming," she was saying as I walked over to her. "Let me introduce you to the crew."

She put out her cigarette and blew smoke at an angle

112

into the air. I met Brad and David, the owners of Pink Panties. Cherry, one of the other dancers was sitting at the bar talking to Grip, the bouncer who was at the door Friday.

"Up in the d.j. booth is Parker Hamilton, better known as D.J. Pump N Hump," she said pointing out.

Everyone was real friendly and said their hellos.

"Heavenly told us you were going to learn how to strip for some guy you like. Let me tell you, you got one of the best dancers in here. Heavenly will help you get that guy's attention," Cherry commented.

Grip spoke up, "I don't know how you don't have his attention now. He must be gay." He said looking me up and down. Brad and David agreed.

"Okay, vultures, get back to work or do something."

Heavenly said joking with the guys, "Come on," she said taking me by the hand. "Let me show you to the dressing room."

After getting changed into my black yoga pants and my black tank top I met Heavenly on stage. She was talking to D.J. Pump N Hump.

"Hey, what's up?" he said when I got close.

"Nothing much," I replied.

"You're in good hands. Heavenly is gonna have you droppin' it like it's hot before you know it," he said laughing.

He was a thin white guy with spiked sandy blonde hair and blue-green eyes. He had a friendly smile.

"Thanks, that's what I hear," I said smiling.

"Pump, give us a few minutes and then we're going to try some of those songs to see which ones she feels comfortable with," Heavenly told him.

"So, what shoes did you bring?"

I had put on some slip-on gym shoes to wear out to the stage. I reached into my bag and brought out the black stilettos I purchased over the weekend.

"Are these okay?" I asked.

"Yeah, girl. Are you going to be able to work those heels? You know those are for the professionals," she smiled.

"I think I can manage," I smiled back. "And before you think I forgot..." I pulled a white envelope out with $1250 in it. I didn't want her to think I wasn't serious.

"You can best believe I didn't forget," she said taking the envelope and counting the money. "Go ahead, put your shoes on and let's get started."

She had me do a few stretches and deep breaths and to walk around the stage to get used to it.

"Are you nervous?" she asked.

"Yes, I am," I said making a slow walk around the stage looking at how high it was and how the brass rail curved around it. "I can't believe I'm actually doing this. I wouldn't have done something like this in a million years before I lost the weight."

"It's nothing to be afraid of. Face the fear is what I always say," she told me. She then had me take center stage and face where the customers would have been sitting had any been there. "Remember, dance is a fine art. No matter what type of dance it is. From ballet to stripping, dance is sensual, relaxing, and full of energy and fun. It's what you make it," Heavenly told me. "So are you ready to get started?"

She had made me feel more relaxed. "Yes, let's get busy."

Heavenly then began to show me basic moves on how to come out from backstage to what to do once I got to the center of the stage. We went over it again and again and then she had D.J. Pump turn on the music so I could practice making my entrance as if I were really performing. We continued working for about an hour and a half.

"Women don't have to be afraid of their bodies or the way their bodies naturally want to move. We are one of

God's greatest creations. You'll be fine." Heavenly was telling me at the end of our practice. "Just make sure you practice, practice, practice."

"Thanks. This was not as bad as I thought once I got use to moving all sexy like that." I had enjoyed my first practice with her. She was nicer than what she portrayed herself to be the first night I met her. We started packing up our things.

"Remember, enjoy the feeling of touching yourself and getting familiar with your body, then grab and hold onto the power," she advised me.

"I think I can do that," I smiled.

"And by the way, you looked like a professional in the heels." She winked at me and gave me a smile.

We said bye to the owners, Grip and Pump. Cherry had left some time ago. We then walked together out to the parking lot.

"Now we can't practice at the club again until Saturday morning. Is that cool with you?" she asked.

"Saturday would be great."

We exchanged phone numbers and left. When I got home I was worn out and ready to jump into a hot bubble bath. I checked to see if I had any messages and there were several on my voicemail, but the one that made my evening was left by Darrius.

Hey, Yanni, I was calling to see what you were doing. Apparently you're somewhere doin' ya thang. Girl, when am I goin' to see ya? I miss hangin' out with ya. Give me a call okay. I want to see ya too girl. Call me. Peace.

"If only he knew how much of me he would soon see me," I said aloud. I then took off my clothes, put my robe on and ran my water for my bath.

A few weeks had passed with Heavenly teaching me

how to strip. Not only had I learned plenty from her, we had become pretty good friends. I learned that Heavenly was really Erica, the college student trying to pay her way through school. She was not only a single parent of a little girl, but she also had to take care of her little brother who was still in high school and who also lived with her. She had told me how her mother had been addicted to crack cocaine and other drugs since she could remember and how one day three years ago her mother just up and left.

"All I know is that I want to provide a better life for my daughter and my brother and if this is what I have to do until I get my degree, then I'll do it," she told me one day when I asked her how she got into stripping. I couldn't do nothing, but respect her. She and I had come up with three songs and different routines for each one. We were trying to come up with ideas for costumes and what would be easy to take off during the routine.

"So no to the nurse's costume?" she asked me.

"I'm just not feeling it, you know. What about the sexy business suit? You don't like that idea?" I shot one of my ideas back at her.

"Hmmm...maybe. I don't know. Let's keep it in mind though. What about a cheerleader outfit?" she asked.

"Maybe. Hey! What about a naughty school girl outfit? You know, I could wear a short plaid skirt with thigh highs and a tight plain white shirt." I was excited about the idea.

"Girl, I love it. You could wear short ruffle panties that peek out from under the skirt and put your hair up in a ponytail then later release it for effect," she sounded pumped about the idea too. "Let's do it!" she said clapping her hands.

We both agreed and gave each other a high five. After our practice we drove over to the adult sex store and shopped for my outfit and other items we thought could be used to spice up the routine. Between my workouts with Greg, my workouts with Heavenly and sticking to my eating plan with Sherri, I was all that, a bag of chips and a red pop to wash it down with. I was so proud of myself. I was so overwhelmed with excitement, I didn't know what to do with myself. I had gone shopping and restocked my closet with cuter, newer and most importantly smaller clothes. New shoes and sandals, new skirts, shirts, dresses and even new panties and bras. With Summer fast approaching, men were coming from out of nowhere trying to talk to me. I didn't know how to handle all of the attention so I just did nothing. Plus, I was going after the man I really wanted, my Darrius. I couldn't help but smile when I thought how close I was to getting him all to myself. I couldn't wait! Heavenly and I had worked out a plan on getting Darrius to Pink Panties to see my performance. Heavenly got me an invitation card shaped like a pair of pink panties that the club owners mail out to their Executive guests. In the invitation Heavenly wrote a note to Darrius saying that his business card had been selected from many that had been dropped in a fishbowl and he was the lucky winner of a special free night at Club Pink Panties. The invitation also stated if he wanted to claim his prize, he had to be at the club this Saturday at 11:00 p.m., ask for Heavenly and tell her the secret phrase, "Big Booties Bounce Better When Bitches Bring Bigger Bank."

"I can't believe you told him that," I said in shock to Heavenly.

"Girl, I think it will be funny hearing him say that," she laughed.

"No. I'm not talking about your little rhyme. I'm talking about you saying he had to be here on Saturday at 11:00." We had discussed an earlier time. "That's when the club is packed and everybody will see me dance."

"Yanni, don't you think he'd find it a bit strange coming to a strip club at noon on a Saturday?"

"Come on, he probably wouldn't even think twice about it," I chimed in.

"Well, remember the club doesn't open until 6:00 in the evening and that's for those old cheap ass men who want to get something for nothing. I mean you know him better than I do, if you think he'd show up here early, then I'll change the time. Just let me know."

She sat and waited patiently for me to answer. She was right. When Darrius went out with his friends to the strip club, they went out even later than 11:00 at night.

"I just didn't think I'd be dancing in front of other men." I was still thrown off by the idea of being naked or damn near naked in front of strangers.

"Girl, you have nothing to worry about. You are good. Plus," she said with a sly smile. "If you're going to be doing this, you might as well make a little change."

I looked at her in shock.

"I can't believe you said that." I playfully pushed her.

"You are looking good and you have become a pro whether you like it or not. You really have gotten good over the few weeks we've been practicing," she said proud of her work.

"Thanks, Heavenly, I needed that," I told her feeling happy with my progress.

"And stop calling me Heavenly, we're friends now," she said.

"Okay, Erica," I smiled.

"Now, let's finish this invitation so we can get it in the mail," she instructed.

Brad and David had agreed on letting me have use of the VIP lounge for my private dance to Darrius. They said they would let me have the room for an hour with no interruptions. I was too nervous as the week went on. I worked out so hard at the gym and with Erica because I had to be perfect for Darrius when I presented my new self to him. Thoughts ran through my mind like will he want to be with me? Am I toned enough? I even wondered if I should not go through with it now and see if I could lose more weight. Erica told me to calm down whenever I told her my concerns and she always reminded me of how far I had come.

"Outside of the weight loss, this is your real reward," she told me after our last practice together. "You got this, girl, you don't have a reason to worry. You've worked hard to get to this point. Remember, face your fears. Now let's go over some last minute tips about the other patrons that will be here." She reminded me that the men were going to make me work for the money.

"They like to feel like they're in control, but what they don't realize is they're paying for an image. You're not going home with them and they're spending damn near their whole paycheck on you," she continued. "They're going to roll their money and place it behind their ears or between their teeth. I showed you how to retrieve it and make them feel like they're king of the world. Remember don't be afraid to let them tuck money in your cleavage or your G-string. They can't really put their little grubby hands on you or Grip or Big Joe will put their hands on them," she laughed.

She was giving me so much information, I just hoped I could remember it all once I got on stage Saturday night. Erica was trying to remind me to act like I was one of the regular dancers here, that way Darrius wouldn't think anything out of the ordinary. I hoped I could pull this off.

The day of the big event I had gone to a day spa and had gotten the works. I got there that morning and didn't leave until that afternoon. I had a bikini wax, an eyebrow wax, a facial, a body scrub, and a massage. I then ate a light lunch with cheesecake for dessert. For the final ser-

119

vice, I got a pedicure and a manicure. I allowed that to be a treat to myself for everything I had accomplished over the last few months. The weight loss, the courage to learn how to strip and the confidence to actually go through with stripping. Also, adding Erica as a new friend and of course, I have to celebrate the fact that tonight I will be with Darrius. How long have I been waiting for this moment. Too damn long. Not only did I feel superb, I looked it too. I now knew I was ready for tonight.

I got to the club at 9:30. I wanted to get there in enough time to get a feel for the atmosphere, to get changed into my costume and to get any last minute tips from Erica. Grip was the first person I saw when I got to the door.

"You ready for your big night?" he asked in his rough voice when he saw me come through the door.

"As ready as I'll ever be," I smiled.

"I saw you perform earlier this week and believe me, babe, you're ready." He gave a hearty laugh and winked at me. I just shook my head and rolled my eyes. He was always flirting with everyone.

"Is Heavenly around?" I asked looking around the club.

It was busy and more customers were coming in even as I was standing there. After Grip searched and patted down the last customer, he answered me.

"Heavenly is in the lap dance room. She should be out shortly. Go to the bar and get you something to drink. Get comfortable and good luck. I'll be looking out for you," He laughed again.

I walked around and spoke to everyone that worked there that I knew. I had met just about everybody who was employed at the club during my practices at one point or another. I waved to D.J. Pump who saw me and beckoned me to come up to the d.j. booth.

"You ready for tonight?" He asked removing his head-sets.

"Yes, I think I am," I replied over the loud music.

"Have you come up with a name?" he asked.

"Oh shit!" I said. Heavenly and I haven't even thought of that. "No, we forgot about that."

"I know you don't want to use your real name. Hey!" he said like he just thought of something good. "What about Storm?"

"Storm?" I asked frowned up.

"Yeah. You were so quiet at first and shy, then BAM!" He jumped towards me. "You surprised us all, just like a storm."

I thought for a minute. I kind of liked it. It did have a ring and a bit of truth to it.

"Plus," he interrupted my thoughts. "You worked with Heavenly." He paused for a minute trying to get me to let it soak in. I wasn't getting it. "Storms come from Heaven. Get it?" he asked smiling and shaking his head. I just laughed.

"All right, Pump, you win. Storm it is. I guess I am ready now. Do you have my music selection?" I asked.

"I have it right here," he said fanning his hand over all of his cd collection.

"Just have it ready for me when I hit the stage," I told him looking at the hundreds of cds he had stored in various cases. I got ready to walk off when he called out to me.

"Storm, if your little boyfriend doesn't show you that he appreciates what you're going to be doing, get with me later and I'll show you how I appreciate it," he winked at me. Once again I had to roll my eyes. At that point, I saw Heavenly come out from the private lap dance area. I waved to her and got her attention.

"Hey, girl, you ready?" she asked hugging me when we got close enough.

"Yeah, I think I'm ready," I said readjusting the duffel bag on my shoulder. "Here." I handed her another white envelope.

"What's this?" she asked looking inside of the envelope.

"It's the other half of the money I owe you," I told her.

"I don't want this," she said giving the money back to me. "We've become more than a business plan. We're friends. You keep this and maybe we can go shopping next week," she smiled and laughed. "Let's go back to the dressing room," she said walking towards the back.

I followed and when I got to the back a few of the other dancers were waiting back there with a cake shaped like a penis and they all yelled, "GOOD LUCK!" I jumped from shock and I couldn't believe it.

"Oh my goodness!" I was too surprised to say anything else. They all hugged me, wished me luck and gave more tips and tricks to get through my performance. They had even given me my own locker which they decorated with small rubber penises, little naked figures having sex and other sex novelty items.

"Of course I had to get you something special," Erica said pulling out a gift bag from her locker.

I looked inside and pulled out the gift. I screamed with laughter.

"Girl you are crazy!" I said cracking up. All the dancers were laughing hard too.

"Well, just in case things don't work out as planned, you will still be satisfied."

She had purchased me a large, black, life-like vibrator. Everybody started clapping and cheering. I laughed so hard.

"Will somebody cut this big dick of a cake?!" Cherry screamed from the back. "I want a piece before I go out for my next set."

"You are a piece!" A dancer they called Jade shouted

out. We all laughed again.

"You're one of us now. You have a locker here and everything," Erica joked giving me a hug.

I thanked her and all the girls for the gifts, the cake and especially the support. They were a cool group of women. I told Erica about the name Pump had given me and explained how he came up with it. She loved it. We then started getting ready for my big debut. I took off my heels, jeans and pull over t-shirt and put on my school girl outfit. After getting dressed I looked in the full length mirror that was near my locker.

"Damn! I look good." I said out loud to myself. I was the only one in the dressing room since all the other girls went back out to work the floor. I was wearing four inch, black, Mary Jane stilettos, plain white thigh-hi's that had a mini bow on the upper back thigh. I had on a very mini, plaid, red and black school girl style skirt with white ruffle panties with red trim peeking from underneath. The white shirt I was wearing was short and tight. It showed off my deep, sexy cleavage. I then pulled all of my hair up to a high ponytail and secured it with a black hair band. I applied my make-up, made sure my backpack was filled with the goodies I'd be using and for the final touch, I put on a satin black scarf with eyes cut out so Darrius couldn't see my face. I had decided that I didn't want him to know it was me until the end of the night. I wanted to see how he would react both before and after he discovered it was his hanging buddy. It was a few minutes before 11:00 and Erica came back to check on me.

"Hey, girl, you ready?" she asked sitting a drink down in front of me at the make-up counter I was sitting in front of. "This is just a little something to calm your nerves," she smiled.

"Thanks," I said taking a sip from the small red straw that was in the glass. "What is this?" I asked taking another sip. It had a fruity taste but with a little kick to it. I couldn't quite pick out what was in it.

"I don't know," Erica replied. "Allen calls it his Nerve Buster Special. He makes it for all the dancers when they're nervous and he never tells what's in it," she said.

"Well, whatever it is, it sure is good," I replied drinking more of it. Allen was one of the bartenders I had also met during one of my practices.

"So, you doing good? You ready?" she asked.

"Yes, I think I am." I took in a deep breath and slowly released it.

"Just remember, men are stimulated visually. If you want to drive Darrius, or any of those men out there crazy, give them fierce attitude and a fierce performance. You run this show. You are the star. Men are here to see you. Take control of your feminine power."

She talked to me like a coach giving his team a last minute pep talk during the last time out of a game. She was right. I had come a long way and I was going to have to perform like my life depended on it. I had to shake these nerves.

"He's here!" Paradise came racing through the door of the dressing room. "He is fine!" she said looking at me smiling. I couldn't even smile back, I was too nervous.

"Look, drink the last of your drink and get yourself together. You can do this," Erica said. "Just be listening for Pump to call your name to take the stage," she said.

And with that, she and Paradise were gone back out onto the floor. I decided to peek out of the dressing room to see if I could see Darrius. I saw Erica just as she got to the door and she and Darrius were saying something. She must have asked him for the password because I could see him dig into his back pocket and pull out the card we had mailed him and read from it. I could see his lips saying, "Big booties bounce better when bitches bring bigger bank." I could also see Erica laugh. She invited him pass Grip and then I also saw Darnell was behind

124

him.

Oh my goodness. I didn't expect him to bring anybody. I whispered to myself. I saw Erica lead both Darrius and Darnell to be seated at the front center stage. She said something else and headed back to me.

"Girl, he is one fine brotha, I must say. I can't believe you ain't said nothing to him after all these years. I don't know how you kept quiet," she said walking to her locker getting a cigarette out. We both sat at the make-up counter. "What did he say?" I asked.

She laughed as she lit her cigarette.

"He cracked me up reading that password I made him say. You should have heard him." She then imitated him stumbling over the words and she laughed again. She continued on. "He is real polite though. I told him congratulations on being tonight's winner and explained to him he would have his own personal stripper for the night. He asked if he could pick her. I told him no, she has already been selected and he would be pleased. I then informed him drinks would be provided for him and he also won an hour in the private lap dance area with his escort of the evening."

"What did he say when you told him that?" I asked anxiously.

"He was like, word, that's straight." She blew smoke towards the ceiling. "His friend was like," 'what about me?'" She rolled her eyes. "I was like, what about you? Just be happy your friend thought enough of you to invite you."

"That's his best friend from way back so he's there for everything, you know," I told her.

"Well, I bet you won't let him be in that private room," she joked.

"Awww hell naw!" I said.

She put her cigarette out. "I'm going back out to check on him and you should be up soon. I'll be up in the d.j. booth with Pump when you go on. Good luck. What am I saying good luck for? You got this. Go do your thing, girl!" She hugged me and was out. A few of the other girls had come back again to wish me luck. What I know was only a few minutes seemed like years before Pump began to introduce me.

"Coming to the stage is one sexy, fly chick. And to our contest winner, this is your personal escort for the night. So please give a holla, a warm welcome and get your dollars ready for...STORM!"

He played a storm in the background with lightening cracking and thunder sounding. Then my first song came on, Mya's *My Love is Like...Woo* from her Moodring cd. By the time Mya had counted off, "1, 2, 3, 4..." I was making my entrance on stage. *Don't be nervous, don't be nervous.* I told myself walking towards center stage. I could see Darrius looking up at me in awe. I had my backpack on and I skipped around stage like I was a little girl getting out of school. After making one trip around the stage, I slowly removed the backpack and left it on the floor for me to get later. *Keep calm, keep calm.* I repeated as I danced around the stage to the other customers first. I looked over at Darrius with an alluring look to let him know that I knew he was our pretend winner. Darnell was giving him pound and cheesing hard like he was the one that was going to be getting with me. So this is how they act when they're in here. Brenda would not be happy with Darnell right about now. *Go slow, take the dollar this guy is holding in his teeth. Go slow, go slow.* I was telling myself. I stayed positioned on the floor of the stage as I danced around for two customers at the same time. I looked on the other side of the stage and saw men calling out to me and waving their money in the air for me to come and get. I made my way around purposely passing Darrius slowly as I went.

My love is like...woo, my kiss is like...woo, my touch is like...woo, my sex is like...woo.

Mya sang as I let one gentleman tuck a dollar into my cleavage. I played with my ponytail, twirling it around one finger and putting a finger from my other hand in my mouth as I danced around for other customers. I stood back up and turned my back towards the men sitting near the stage and bent over so they could see my ruffle panties looking back at them. I laid on my back and faced them as I raised my legs into the air an opened them up like a wide V. Men began to throw money between my legs as I rubbed my pussy up and down for their viewing pleasure. After I collected more money I finally went to the center stage and looked directly at Darrius as the song was ending. I leaned my back onto the pole and slowly slid down with my legs slowly opening as I went down. I threw my head to the side, closed my eyes and put my hand between my legs and touched my pussy, pretending to play with it. Darrius took a big gulp of his drink. I knew he was probably drinking McCallins on the rocks. Nothing but top shelf scotch for him, that's all he ever drank. Darnell threw a few bills my way as my next song came on.

D.J. Pump and Hump put on R. Kelly's *Imagine That.* This got Darrius' attention because I knew this was one of his favorite songs. I slowly begin to unbutton my shirt and let my red, lacey bra show. I crawled over to Darrius after I removed my shirt and put it around his neck as I gave him a kiss on the cheek. I could smell his Ermenegildo Ziegan cologne. He always wore expensive, designer cologne. It was a blend of cashmere wood and patchouli. He smelled so sexy. I almost lost focus. "Use your feminine power." I could hear Erica in my head telling me. I stood up, sauntered over to the pole to do a slow, sexy basic swing. "Pivot on right foot, grab pole

with left hand, hook the back of your left ankle around
the pole, push off hard with right foot, go around clock-
wise," I could hear Erica's instructions guiding me as I
slowly went around the pole like I had been doing it all
my life. I watched the room spin around and everyone's
eyes were on me. I slid down the pole until my feet
touched the floor. I crawled over to Darrius again, stood
up and slowly removed my skirt. I let it fall at my feet
and kicked it into his lap. I was now standing in front of
him with nothing on but my red bra and my white and
red trimmed panties. I took my thumbs on each side of
the rim of the panties and slowly, slowly pushed them
down until they were at my feet. *Stay steady, stay steady.*
You are not going to fall. You are not going to fall. I kept saying to myself. I bent down with my legs opened, scooped
up the panties, sniffed them and ran them up and down
his body and let them rest on his shoulder. He just
looked me up and down and took in a deep breath. I
could tell he was quite pleased. I then got up and I was
now wearing black G-string panties, white thigh-hi's and
my red bra. I danced around a few more times for the
other customers and collected more money. Lying on my
back doing a sexy dance, making my ass jiggle, dropping
it like it was hot, and I was making each customer feel
like he was the king for the night. I gave alluring looks,
smiled, teased and played with them all. The customers
all approved by dropping more bills on the stage, tucked
my G-string or tossed money playfully at my feet. The
big finale of the show was coming, so I prepared for it. I
crawled back to Darrius, turned my back towards him,
reached behind my back and unsnapped my bra. I let the
bra fall as I kept my hands over my breasts turning back
to face him. I cradled my breasts across my left arm as I
stroked them with my right hand like it was a kitten. I
then got close enough to grab his head and slowly rub his
face into my breasts. I could feel him kiss each nipple,

keeping them hard. I then pushed his head back to finish up the act and ended in front of Darrius, on my knees, leaning back on my back with my nipples pointing straight up in the air. Everyone in the club broke out cheering. I couldn't believe I did it. Erica then came out on stage and helped me collect the rest of the money and my clothes. Once we got back to the dressing room we both screamed and hugged each other.

"Girl, you did wonderful!" she said shouting and jumping up and down. "You should have seen the way everybody was looking at you." She was so excited. I was trying to catch my breath and get my robe on too.

"Did I do good?" I asked still slightly nervous.

"You did so much better than good! I am so proud of you!" she said eyes wide.

I had to sit down and just try to grasp on to what had just happened. Some of the other dancers came back to the dressing room.

"Girl, you did yo thang!" one said coming in giving me a high five.

"You sure you ain't done this before?" Another asked jokingly.

"Damn girl! All the men are requesting you for private dances," someone else said.

"Good job!" another dancer said. I just thanked everyone and took it all in.

"You ready to do your private dance for Darrius?" Erica asked.

"I need to get changed into the other outfit," I said getting up to go to my locker.

"I'll go and make sure the room is empty and everything is set," she said helping me get out the other outfit.

"I'll be getting dressed then."

She left and quickly got changed. I removed my G-string and slipped into another school girl skirt. This one was all red. I left the thigh-hi's on along with the Mary

129

Jane stilettos. I then put on a half top that read "Bad Girl" on the front. Just as I was making sure the satin mask was on tight enough and my make-up was cool, Erica came back in.

"You look good Yanni. He is up in the VIP room waiting for you. We got him another drink and he's just chillin," she reported.

"Did he say anything?" I asked.

"He was asking when did we hire you and who are you. He was saying he's seen plenty of women dance before but none like you. You blew his mind girl!" she laughed.

"Thanks to you," I told her.

"Yeah, well, you did learn from the best," she said acting like she was popping her collar. "Now don't be taking all day getting up there," he said handing me my backpack. "Your man awaits you."

I put my backpack on and headed to the private room.

"Good job." Big Joe, the other bouncer told me as I got to the red curtains to go back into the VIP room.

"Thanks. I was nervous as hell," I told him.

"You did excellent. Don't worry." He then parted the curtains for me to go back. I walked down the long hallway to get to where Darrius was. He was sitting on the caramel colored loveseat, sipping his drink when I appeared in the doorway.

"Wow, you really did good out there," he said.

I just stood in the doorway not saying anything. I was taking him all in. He was wearing his dark denim jeans that were slightly baggy. Not too much though. Darrius liked to be in style but he didn't agree with the sagging pants or the thug look. He had on a multi-colored stripped button down long sleeve shirt. I could tell it was from the designer Ralph Lauren because it had the jockey and horse symbol on the front breast pocket. He had on a pair of the new Lacoste Revolve sport shoes, white leather with aqua blue trim. I know those costs about $140 and I do remember him telling me his food distribution business was going well, but damn I didn't know it was going that well! I removed my backpack, took out a cd and put it in the wall mounted Bose. He spoke again.

"So are you new here?"

I still didn't answer. I didn't want him to recognize my voice so I just kept silent. I hit the play button and my first song came on. It was Aaliyah's, *I Care for You*. I made my way over to him, sprinkling red and pink rose petals on him I got from my backpack. I then straddled him and rubbed my body all over his. I noticed he not only had a fresh haircut, but he also had a new earring. This was much bigger than the last one I saw him wearing. It was a diamond stud and it looked like it could be about a carat. "Damn!" I thought. His Zegna cologne was intoxicating. My nipples were getting as hard as his dick had become and I could hear his breathing pattern change.

"Damn, baby, you feel good!" he whispered in my ear.

I continued to keep quiet and caress his body. I then unbuttoned his shirt and let his massive chest be exposed. I could tell he's been working out more too since the last time I saw him. I reached into my bag for some massage oil. He completely removed his shirt when he saw what I had. His sandy complexion body glistened as I rubbed oil on his large shoulders, down his chest and onto his muscular arms. After rubbing the oil into him, I got a large black feather out of my bag and playfully glided it all over his body.

"Tell me your real name, Storm," he said between deep breaths.

I still didn't answer. I looked deep into his eyes. My nerves had just about gone. He stared back.

"Something about your eyes looks familiar," he said.

I quickly looked away and stood up from him. My

next song then came on, perfect timing. It was *Would You Mind* by Janet Jackson from her All for You cd. I then begin my dance for Darrius. I let my ponytail down and my hair fell in place around my face. I pulled my half top over my head and let my breasts be out for his pleasure. Darrius reached up to take them in his hands. I was standing between his legs and I turned my back to him, slid my skirt down and bent over so he could get a view of my pleasure spot. I could feel him run his hands over my ass.

"Damn, you look so good," he said.

I couldn't wait any longer, I unfastened his pants and got on top of him and let his swollen dick penetrate my inner walls. I let out a deep moan as he entered me. I passionately kissed him and let my pussy do what it wanted. He was stroking me deep and grabbing my hair. He whispered into my ear, "Let me see who you are." As he reached for my satin mask. I pulled away and begin kissing his neck and sucking on his ears. He moaned telling me how he liked that. I grabbed a can of whipped cream out of my pack and sprayed it over my tits and let him lick it off. I wanted him to fuck the shit out of me. So I lightly whispered, just enough for him to hear, "Fuck me, please." I moaned in his ear. That was all it took. He laid my back onto the loveseat and began to stroke me deeper and deeper as he nibbled and bit on my titties. I moaned with pleasure. I couldn't contain my emotions and began to scream lightly as I played with his nipples and took in all of his love muscle. He felt better than I ever imagined. His dick was thick and fit just right in my wet pussy.

"You like this?" he asked hitting my pussy with force so strong he was making me stutter when I did try to speak.

"Y-y-yes." I finally said. "Fuck me. Take me, Darrius!" I whispered.

We switched positions and he was fucking me doggie style. He felt so good and his dick was so strong. He was so deep inside of me, fucking me slow then fast. He was licking and sucking the back of my neck and sending chills throughout my body. He reached around and squeezed my swinging breasts. I reached down and played with my clit. I was so damn wet you could hear the squishy sound as he thrust in and out of me. He slapped my ass with his big, powerful hand and that sent electricity to my pussy. I was ready to cum, but I didn't want to until I knew for sure he was ready. We both kept it up until we could no longer take it. Before I knew it, I was cumming all over his manly dick. He was grunting and cumming in me too.

"Shit! Shit!" I screamed as I creamed and released on him.

"Damn baby!" he replied. "Damn!"

Afterwards, I grabbed wet wipes and towels out of my pack and cleaned us up. He pulled his pants up and fastened his shirt as I put my top and my skirt back on. I still hadn't said anything. The cd with other slow jams continued to play as I sat next to him on the couch.

"I guess you're still not going to say anything," he said waiting for me to respond and taking a sip of his drink. I said nothing. "That's cool. I like the mystery of it all," he smiled. "Your body is banging," he stated looking me up and down. "You feel good too, inside and out." He laughed trying to make conversation. I was trying to figure how I was going to reveal who I was to him. "You got a man?" he asked. I shook my head no.

"You have got to be kidding me. Some brotha somewhere is pissed because you're not at home with him right now. I mean, if you were my woman for one, you wouldn't be out here dancing in no club. And two, we'd be back at my place, making love," he said smiling and taking my hand in his. "You wouldn't even be thinking

133

about doing a job like this, because I would spoil you so much you wouldn't want another man looking at you. I'd massage your sexy body every night. I'd make sure you knew you were a woman.".

I laughed because I know Darrius does treat his women well. He always has. That's just him. He likes making sure a woman is treated like a queen and that's one of the many reasons why I always had a crush on him.

"Hey, I got you to laugh. Why don't you let me see who you are?" he asked reaching for the satin mask. This time I didn't pull away. He pulled the satin scarf from over my eyes. "Yanni?" He said in shock. "What the fuck?" He sat looking stunned.

"Yes, it's me, Darrius," I said.

"But...I don't understand. Your body...what are you doing stripping? What's going on?" He stumbled over his words.

I explained to him the forever crush I've had on him and how I came to the conclusion to lose weight for him. I told him about the workouts, the nutritionist I had hired and the lies I had told to him about why I wasn't coming around. I explained to him about this plan and how I met and hired Heavenly to teach me how to strip and get him here to the club. I just told him everything.

"Damn, Yanni! I really didn't know that you felt like that about me." He threw his arms around me. "You look good now girl, I mean damn, look at you." He leaned in to kiss me. His lips felt so warm and soft. The lips that I've always wanted to kiss, lick and suck on. I pulled away.

"What's wrong, Yanni?" he asked. Before I could answer he commented again. "Yanni, you look fine as hell now girl!" He grinned harder looking me up and down.

"That's just it." I said. "I look good to you now, but I'm still the same Yanni. If I couldn't get your attention

134

me asking me for a private dance. I told them I was scheduled to do a few bachelor parties, I wasn't able to stick around. When Erica and I got out to the parking lot, Darrius was parked next to my car. He jumped out of his ride.

"You need any help?" He asked taking a bag from me.

"Damn, it sure is Yanni!" Darnell said leaning out the window. "Girl, you look hell-a-fied good! What did you do with yourself?"

"Darnell, man shut up!" Darrius turned to him and yelled.

"I'm going to go pull my car around, you gonna be okay?" Erica asked.

"I'll be fine. I'll follow you once I get done." She headed to her car.

"I need to tell you I'm sorry, Yanni." Darrius said. "I really didn't know how you felt about me."

"The signs were always there, but because I didn't fit into the image you've created for the type of women you want to deal with, you never noticed." I told him.

"You're right. Then I was very insensitive about your weight loss. Instead of telling you how good you looked period, because you've always looked good, I told you how good you look now and I'm sorry for saying that the way I did."

"Apology accepted." I said hugging him.

"So can I take you out sometime?" He said kissing me on my forehead.

"As friends." I smiled. "As friends."

By that time Erica pulled up and honked her horn. "You ready, girl?" She shouted out the window.

"Yeah, I'm on my way."

I told both Darrius and Darnell bye and I'd see them later. I realized I am proud of myself for so many reasons on so many different levels. I'm happy about losing the weight, about taking on various challenges, about facing fears

and for having enough self esteem to not just accept anything because I had no other choice. It feels good to be in
a position where I have an option now and for always. I
have that feminine power. Now, time for those hot wings
and fries!

with who I was inside why should I want your attention with who I've become outside?" I stood up halfway disappointed. I couldn't believe I did all of this for him. I should have done this a long time ago for myself.

"Yanni, I'm sorry. I didn't mean it like that," he said taking me by my arm.

"Yes, you meant it, Darrius, and you know what? I'm not even upset that you said it. I'm glad that I finally had this fantasy moment with you. Now I can stop imagining and go out and get me a real life. Who knows, I may just find a man who wants me for my body and my brain. Don't trip, 'cause I'm not. We'll always be friends." With that, I gathered my things and headed down to the dressing room.

"How did it go?" Erica said rushing up to me.

"It went." I said getting out of my costume.

"What happened?" she said sounding shocked. "Didn't things go well?"

"I just realized I should have done this weight loss shit for myself!" I said crying.

"Did he do something to you?" she asked sounding angered.

"No, nothing like that. I just had a moment when I realized I should have believed in myself more and did what I had to do for me, because of me. You know what I mean?" I wiped my eyes with tissue she handed me.

"I think I do. You want to get out of here and go get something to eat," she asked.

"I haven't had greasy wings and fries for awhile," I said.

"Good I know the perfect spot for some hot wings," she said. "Get dressed, I'm going to see if Brad or David is around so I can get off."

In the meantime I got my jeans, heels and t-shirt back on. I waited as Erica got dressed since David gave her the rest of the night off. We got all the gifts, cake, and clothes packed and headed to the car. I said my good-byes to everyone and promised to stop back in for a visit sometime. I had a lot of men stopping me asking me for a private dance. I told them I was scheduled to do a few bachelor parties, I wasn't able to stick around. When Erica and I got out to the parking lot, Darrius was parked next to my car. He jumped out of his ride.

"You need any help?" he asked taking a bag from me.

"Damn, it sure is Yanni!" Darnell said leaning out the window. "Girl, you look hell-a-fied good! What did you do with yourself?"

"Darnell, man shut up!" Darrius turned to him and yelled.

"I'm going to go pull my car around. You gonna be okay?" Erica asked.

"I'll be fine. I'll follow you once I get done." She headed to her car.

"I need to tell you I'm sorry, Yanni," Darrius said. "I really didn't know how you felt about me."

"The signs were always there, but because I didn't fit into the image you've created for the type of women you want to deal with, you never noticed," I told him.

"You're right. Then I was very insensitive about your weight loss. Instead of telling you how good you looked period, because you've always looked good. I told you how good you look now and I'm sorry for saying that the way I did."

"Apology accepted," I said hugging him.

"So, can I take you out sometime?" he asked kissing me on my forehead.

"As friends," I smiled. "As friends." By that time Erica pulled up and honked her horn.

"You ready, girl?" she shouted out the window.

"Yeah, I'm on my way." I told both Darrius and Darnell bye and I'd see them later. I realized I am proud of myself for so many reasons on so many different levels. I'm happy about losing the weight, about taking on various challenges, about facing fears and for having enough self esteem to not just accept anything because I had no other choice. It feels good to be in a position where I have an option now and for always. I have that feminine power. Now, time for those hot wings and fries!